BACK ON CHEAT

Stories of West Virginia

GARRISON PHILLIPS

For information please contact:

Garrison Phillips

E-mail address: garri1@earthlink.net

Previously Published

Happy Easter* in *The Storyteller

River with the Banks Falling In* in *Apalachee Review

ISBN 978-1530580781

Book design and production by Bramble Books
info@bramblebooks.com

Text font: Fairfield Light, 12 point
Title font: Luna, 24 point

Cover Photo: © Strekoza2 | Dreamstime.com
High Falls on Shavers Fork Photo: © Harris Shiffman | Dreamstime.com

Printed in United States of America

The paper used in this publication meets the minimum requirements of

American National Standard for Information Sciences—
Permanence of Paper for Printed Library Materials, ANSI Z39.48-1984

Table of Contents

Acknowledgments ____ vi

Happy Easter ____ 1

Grit ____ 7

Issac and the Widow Duerr ____ 19

Homer ____ 61

The Snyders of Pine Hollow ____ 91

D-Day ____ 103

Pages from a Memoir ____ 119

August 2, 1953 ____ 129

River with the Banks Falling In ____ 151

Trailing Arbutus ____ 163

Maple Marinade ____ 179

Bringing Home the Colors ____ 189

Acknowledgments

I am grateful to the late Sanford (Sandy) Friedman, award winning author of *Totem Pole*, as the first person to encourage me to write more than letters of protest. I was a member for a few of the twenty-two years that he led his exciting writing group in New York City. It began at SAGE and then moved to Sandy's Greenwich Village apartment. It was free. No fee. When I began my first story he told me, "Go home and read *To Kill A Mockingbird* and Katherine Anne Porter's *Noon Wine* once again before you write another word. Then perhaps you'll understand the need to capture the special cadence for your West Virginia stories." I did as he asked.

My thanks to Dorothy Calo and John Barrow of Sandy's group who remain loyal friends and critics;

To Tom Kamber, the founder of OATS (Older Adults Technology Services), that teaches the Internet free to seniors, for suggesting that I write a blog for them; eight years later *Everyday Strolls* is still going strong with the technical help and enthusiasm of Renee Martinez and Kimberly Brennsteiner;

Old friend and fellow activist, Michael Alenyikov (*Ivan and Misha*) who keeps me on my toes from California via e-mails;

GayWrites and the extraordinary group of writers in The Monday Group that I have been fortunate to join here in Fort Lauderdale;

The late Warren Day, who was co-producer of the Peter Jennings News Hour and was the basis for the first year of the TV series, *Murphy Brown*, challenged me as no one else had with my writing. Under his careful eye, I learned so very, very much. Thank you, Warren. You are greatly missed every single day.

Back On Cheat would not have been completed without the editing skills of my dear friend, Joanne Lewis–attorney, gifted writer with five published books to her credit (*The Forbidden Room* (book one of a trilogy), *The Lantern, Make Your Own Luck,*

Michelangelo and Me (a five book series), and *Wicked Good*), and Marjetta Geerling (Broward College professor of creative writing and author of *Fancy White Trash*) with her meticulous proof reading. I am indebted to both Joanne and Marjetta for their fine work and encouragement to keep writing;

And to Gary T. Smith for his suggestions as he read some early drafts.

Lastly, Larry Bramble, a man of many talents. An accomplished actor and fine director, his careful publishing skills and insightful design leave nothing to be desired.

Happy Easter

It had begun to snow lightly as I passed through Maryland, but now it had turned into quite a storm. Most unusual as this was early April and I was driving in to celebrate Easter. I have been returning to my hometown of Elkins, West Virginia for over fifty years. It has become almost a monthly event. In the beginning it was to visit, then to aid in the care of my grandmother and, finally, my mother.

Driving in from the east you must traverse five mountains, three of them over 4,000 feet high. The mountains are a formidable obstacle filled with tall timber and a tangled undergrowth of laurel and rhododendron. To this day, folks tell tales and discuss the amazing journey of the early settlers who crossed these barriers mostly on foot and leading a pack mule. One of the local histories tells of a man who carried his crippled wife on his back into Randolph County from the South Branch. Strapped to her back was their only utensil, an iron skillet, and their one tool, an ax. Strung around her neck were two bags holding precious salt. Their only other possession on this journey into the forests to make a new beginning was his gun.

Having safely traversed Allegheny, Rich, Cheat, and Middle Mountains, I slowly drove onto the four lane expressway whose six miles or so would take me into Elkins. This expressway was originally the hoped for new road across the mountains to

Virginia. But the engineers had given up because of the terrain, and only six miles had been completed.

Now I was battling a truly heavy storm, and I slowed to a crawl as I approached the last few miles of my drive into Elkins. As I eased forward through what had become a blinding blizzard, a halted pickup truck suddenly loomed out of the swirling snow. Beside it was a man wildly waving, his arms swinging in an arc over his head. His appearance was so sudden, blurred by the storm, I passed by before realizing that it was a plea for help. I stopped, shifted into reverse, and began to slowly back up to the pickup truck.

Opening my door, I hung out the side of my car in order to maneuver because the snow had become so heavy it blocked my rear window. Backing ever so slowly, I stopped beside the truck and suddenly the passenger door was pulled open and the man jumped into my car.

"Hey, Mister, thank you. Broke down," he blurted out.

"Where you headed?" I asked.

"Elkins. Just this side at the Seneca Garage. My brother-in-law's a mechanic there." This all came out in a mumble of words, barely audible to me.

He turned to face me, nodded as though to say, "Go ahead," and closed the door. He was a giant of a man, and his presence filled the passenger side of the front seat of my car. He appeared to be in his late twenties or so, dressed in work boots, bib overalls, a red and black checked lumber jacket, and a matching cap. Spilling out from around his cap was a mass of red curls. His eyes were watery blue and stared out of a ruddy complexioned face splotched with splashes of deep red. I didn't know if his coloring was from cold or drink, for now I detected a strong odor which I took to be the sweet, overpowering smell of rum.

Reaching with my left hand under my seat, I touched the hammer I carry there for reassurance. Fortunately, I have not had to defend myself since the Army training days, and I have always been sure that if I were mugged in the Big Apple, I would hand over everything without argument, even though gritting my teeth at having to comply. Yet here I was, driving through a raging storm with a stranger who might just do me harm and all due to my Good Samaritan action. I felt helpless and ever so stupid.

A few years past, one of my former college classmates had been driving in to Elkins to visit his ailing father when he picked up a hitchhiker on Cheat Mountain. As the hitchhiker entered my friend's car, two accomplices suddenly appeared from out of the woods. They left my classmate, badly beaten, along side the highway and he ended up sharing his father's hospital room. I spoke with him a few years ago and he said, "Yeah, they could have had the car. As it is, I have a bum left eye and wear glasses with a special lens. The car was abandoned in Pocahontas county, stripped of everything with any value. No more helping hitchhikers for me."

Nervous as a cat, I started driving quickly forward, thinking, *What have I done? This could all be a trick. He could have a buddy hiding in the truck.* I plowed through the deepening snow far faster than I should to put some distance between my car and the pickup.

He glanced at me with a look of surprise as I sped forward. He had removed his cap and sat hunched with it clutched in his hands.

A quarter of a mile or so further, I slowed and proceeded with more caution. Apparently no one was following me for, glancing in my side mirror, I could see no lights behind me.

In the ominous silence, I chatted about myself. "I grew up in Elkins. Went to high school there."

He grunted in reply.

I continued. "My folks have been in Randolph County for a long time."

Again no verbal response although this time I distinctly heard a low, rumbling sort of groan.

"Now I live in New York City, but I'm driving in for the Easter weekend."

Silence. He was leaning forward, squinting through the windshield.

"My grandmother was ninety-six in February, and we're celebrating a little late." I was chattering away like the very nervous man that I was and the palms of my hands were wet with sweat as I gripped the wheel.

He half turned to me with a twisted smile and a nod of his head.

Getting him to speak was apparently not going to happen, so I shut up and concentrated on driving. Two miles or so seemed to inch by as I silently prayed to see the lights of Elkins. As we approached the Seneca Garage the man started to fiddle with the door handle. Closer to civilization, I no longer felt as threatened but his silence annoyed me, and now he appeared ready to jump out of the car before I had even stopped. As I braked and pulled slowly into the garage driveway under the bright, neon lights, he leaped out of the car and ran to the side of the parking lot, leaving the car door wide open to the cold and snow.

As I came to a full stop, shifting into park, he was quickly back, poking his head into the open doorway, grinning broadly.

Wiping his mouth and chin with his weathered hand, he explained quickly, his words piling on one another in his obvious joy, "Mister, I sure do thank ya. I didn't want to say much 'cause I had a big chaw of tobacco, and I was afraid of dribblin' on your pretty car. Comin' in to get Easter baskets for my little girls. I been laid off since last fall and all we could do for Christmas was cut a tree. But the mill is workin' again, and I got paid today so we can celebrate a little."

Grinning at him in relief, I happily replied, "You're welcome. Hope you get your truck fixed okay." I had mistaken the sweet tobacco smell for rum. My instinct had been right to stop to help someone after all, although it went against my rule-of-thumb policy of no hitchhikers.

“Oh, my brother-in-law’ll help me.” He was fairly bursting with energy. “You have a nice Easter with your grandma. And, Mister, I thank ya. I do thank ya. I would’ve had to walk all the way in but for you.”

“Happy Easter to you,” I replied, silently thanking the powers that be that I had stopped to give him a ride.

He closed the door and stood there, a great bear-of-a-man, snowflakes catching on his eyelashes, glistening on his hair and rough lumber jacket. He still clutched his cap in his hand while he waved goodbye to me. “Happy Easter, Mister. Happy Easter.”

Flashing my lights in response, I pulled out of the Seneca Garage driveway. Maneuvering slowly back onto the road, I drove carefully towards my mother’s house on Robert E. Lee Avenue and, indeed, a happy Easter.

Grit

It was late one grey November afternoon when Mark shambled into the tavern courtyard in Winchester. Clutching a cane, he was a tired, frail shadow of the brave volunteer who had gone off to fight the British in 1779. He leaned against the door, fumbling at the latch but was unable to open it. Exhausted, Mark sank onto the stoop, his cane clutched tightly in his fist.

Caleb had just stepped out of the woodlot across the street, his arms full of kindling, when he saw the tattered soldier slumped against the tavern door. It took only a moment for him to realize the ghostly figure was his father. He whispered, "Daddy," letting the kindling fall to the ground and ran to help. Caleb slipped his arms around his father, murmuring over and over, "Daddy, Daddy, Daddy." Crying outright, he led his father, slowly, step by step to the bench beside the tavern doorway.

"Caleb, Caleb, is that you?" Mark questioned as he reached to touch Caleb's face.

Caleb took his father's frail hand and brushed his lips across his fingers. "Yes, oh, yes," he murmured through tears of joy as he pressed his face against his father's hand. He could feel the bony frame of his father through the rags of an army coat. It seemed to Caleb that he was holding a bundle of sticks.

A year ago, when Caleb turned twelve, he learned his father was taken prisoner. A returning wounded neighbor brought the news of Mark's capture in a raid by British cavalry. It had been such a long, anguished wait not knowing whether his father survived the war. And now, he was here, nestled in his embrace.

Caleb looked up as Mistress Hardy appeared in the doorway sternly demanding, "What is it?" She quickly recognized Mark. "Oh, God. It's you." She knelt beside him on the bench, her arms reaching to embrace both Mark and Caleb.

That evening, after bathing, a hot meal, and some rest, Mark was celebrated as a hero by many of the tavern's patrons. Old friends had quickly been summoned and now surrounded Mark as he tiredly greeted them, one by one. With his left arm encircling Caleb, Mark repeatedly touched the boy's face or hair, pulling him close again and again as reassurance that his son was truly beside him. Mark was not up to much, and soon Caleb tucked him into the freshly made pallet in the little room on the first floor of the tavern that was their home

In the days and weeks to come as Mark slowly regained his health, he met almost nightly with other veterans in a small back room of the tavern. There, they exchanged stories of the war, of their hopes and plans for the future, and the prayer for some pay for their services.

"The new government has no money. There will be no pay, mark my words." This sad but true comment came from Mr. Whitman. He owned a print shop and news had a way of making its way to him before the others.

Mark said little of his imprisonment to Caleb but talked often to others of what he had endured as a prisoner of the hated Red Coats.

Caleb overheard his father and the other soldiers as he eavesdropped when he was thought to be asleep. He had enlarged a tiny knothole in the wall of the little room, which enabled him to view and hear in the flickering candlelight the accounts of the men as they were served tankards of ale by Mistress Hardy.

He spent night after night watching and listening as the men talked, often until dawn, relating their trials and triumphs in the Revolution. One night, he heard his father bitterly recount the four long months he had spent in the hold of a prison ship in New York harbor as the other men listened, shaking their heads, wiping away tears.

"Those were months without proper food and filthy conditions." His father fingered the handle of a beer mug. "Raw meat was rationed in the afternoon. Too late to be cooked as we were locked below deck in the evening. We ate the meat raw or held it overnight with hope we might be able to cook the next day. Once locked below we had no access to water and what water the Red Coats provided was thick with scum and not fit for a dog. Loyal New Yorkers rowed out to give us what they could. Sometimes, just dry corn which we softened to swallow by holding the hard kernels in our mouths. Those who died during the night could not be removed until the next day. Disease was rampant but the worst was no water." His father took a swig of beer and appeared as if he wasn't able to continue.

Mr. Whitman finished the story. "It was unspeakable. The British ignore the reports of these horrid conditions. I hear from New York that three out of four prisoners died on those prison ships and more were lost on the ships than were actually killed in battle. Sad, sad indeed. And forget about compensation for the brave men who made it home. The government has no money to pay them." Mr. Whitman paused, drawing every man's attention. Then, in his booming voice, he continued. "Fortunately, there is land stretching from Canada to the Carolinas. Land to be granted to you all, the veterans, for your service. Who better than former soldiers to settle and secure these lands from the Indian raids, to clear the forests and to grow dirt patches into villages and towns as the frontier is pushed further and further west? It will build a broader tax base for every state and all will prosper. So, who better for this task than soldiers who defeated the hated Red Coats?"

The men applauded and cheered, banging tankards on the tavern's tables. Caleb tingled with excitement as he watched and listened, first his eye and then his ear pressed close against the knot hole.

In the two years since the war's end, Mark had worked hard, saving and speaking daily to Caleb of the proposed move to the Tygart Valley. "So many forms, so many signatures, to qualify," Mark lamented. "Signatures of commanding officers are required as proof of service as well as pay records and have to be available which requires the approval of local officials. So we wait for the forms to be reviewed and finally approved in Williamsburg. We wait. I will be notified in care of Colonel Humphrey in the Tygart Valley." Mark grinned and ruffled Caleb's hair. "Not to despair, we will do this. This is my dream. Our future. Some day soon you will be a landowner, and the world will be yours."

It was more than his father's goal to settle in the Tygart Valley that fired Caleb's excitement about the planned journey to the west. He could leave behind the years of yearning for both his parents. His life with Mistress Hardy was rich and filled with her love. However, Caleb was far happier in the woods or tending Mr. Manner's sheep. His fingers came alive with the touch of his traps, carefully baited and skillfully hidden along the river bank. His father's long time friend, Mr. Callahan, who had continued to teach him trapping skills during his father's absence, told everyone, "The boy possesses a special knack for setting the traps. He's a natural woodsman."

Caleb was a good student and recited his lessons dutifully to Mistress Hardy. But it was the heft of a gun and the acrid smell of burnt gunpowder that thrilled his senses, not the tedium of a careful script on his slate tablet.

At last, in the spring of 1786, Mark and Caleb began preparing for their long awaited journey to the Tygart Valley. The two of them immediately began to stock needed goods and their little room became cramped as the days passed.

To Caleb, when he looked back at the last thirty-six hours, it was like a stabbing, brutal storm that stuck without warning. There had been no threatening, dark clouds, no rolling thunder, or bright flashes of lightning. It had all happened so quickly. He had returned from an errand and found his father stretched out and fully clothed on his pallet in their room surrounded by the supplies for the journey to their new lives. His father's face was gray, and the skin drawn taut across his cheekbones. He was burning with fever. That night the raging fever drained his energy and bathed him in a continual, cold sweat.

Caleb recalled holding his breath as he attempted to steady his shaking hand when he spooned Mistress Hardy's broth to his father's tight lips.

"Just a sip. Please take a sip," Caleb begged.

For two long nights, Caleb sat with his father, doing what he could to make him comfortable, to ease his pain, encouraging him to drink the hot broth. Two days and Caleb was worn out for he had slept only fitfully, waking often to gaze at his father in the flickering light of the candles.

Caleb replayed his father's final words. They were spoken, not to Caleb or to Mistress Hardy who was in the room, but to Caleb's long departed mother. "Help me," his father had called suddenly in a loud clear voice as he reached out his hand. His fingers grasped air as a smile crossed his face. A smile which to Caleb's amazement appeared to erase the tired lines of illness.

"Oh, Celia, thank you, thank you," he said and then he was gone. His words lost in the space of the dim, candle lit room.

"Ah, dear Celia. She was here to help him make the crossing." Mistress Hardy pressed her handkerchief tight against her eyes. "Poor cousin Celia, taken before her time as well. And now they are together. Oh, my dear boy." She pulled Caleb into her arms, rocking him gently.

Caleb sat quietly; no words would ease the loss. He watched as Mistress Hardy summoned her porter. With the aid of men called from the main room of the tavern, they gently removed Mark's body.

Caleb knelt beside the gravesite, his hands clasped tightly together as he watched the slow lowering of his father's casket into the ground. Then it was done. Finished. Silence filled the graveyard. It became so quiet it seemed to Caleb that even the birds stopped singing. The droning of the simple prayer of the good parson signaled the grating sound of the shovels as they dug into the pile of earth beside the grave. The sudden spatter of dirt as it fell onto the rough, wooden box began gently and then grew louder and louder, finally drowning out all thought from Caleb's mind. It was a sound which he would remember all his life.

"Come on, Caleb," Mistress Hardy said. "We're done here."

Softly, he whispered, "Yes, ma'am." Caleb took her hand, rose slowly, and allowed Mistress Hardy to lead him from the gravesite.

Once at the tavern, he stood in the middle of the small room he had shared with his father. Gear, food, tools, and other items for their journey to Tygart Valley crowded around him.

"What do I do now?" Caleb asked the air.

He looked around the room, at his father's pallet, all they had collected. Slowly, the answer came to him.

Caleb sat at one end of the long table facing his father's friends and associates, including Mr. Whitman and pastor Dean. Mistress Hardy arranged for the gathering the week following Mark's passing. Out of respect and loyalty to Caleb's father, they had agreed to help the young man. As they greeted Caleb, more than one pressed a coin or sometimes two or even three into his hands. Caleb tried to protest the men's generosity, but they insisted.

"He was due these," Mr. Whitman said. "Aye, due these as well as my gratitude for his fine work. Such a man with figures. He saved me money with his sound advice and caught errors in the billing of my accounts. An honorable man and a brave soldier. He'll be missed. Greatly missed." Mr. Whitman put his hand on Caleb's shoulder. "You're not ready for this journey, boy. You need more schooling. Learn figures and be like your father."

"You're tall, and you have a strong back," Parson Dean said, "but you have the face of a babe."

"An angel is what he is." Mistress Hardy shook the sleeve of Caleb's blouse. "And a stubborn one at that. I've been telling him for days that it's too dangerous, and he's not ready."

"You don't know a thing about farming. Or do you, young man?" the Parson asked, holding a Bible in one hand and a mug of cider in the other.

"Listen to the Pastor," Mr. Whitman said. "Your father always did."

The men grew silent for the moment, sipping their cider as they awaited Caleb's response.

Caleb stammered, "I know some about farming. I've helped with Mr. Manner's sheep. I can shear and I know good pasture and..." Caleb's voice faltered.

"But crops. What do you know of that? The Bible tells us there is a time to plant and a time to pluck up that which is planted. Do you know the when and how of that?"

"Tell us what you know," Mr. Whitman chimed in.

"When is the best time to plant corn?" a farmer asked.

"What do you do if grasshoppers start eating your wheat?" Mr. Callahan persisted.

Caleb glanced at the men around him, taking a moment to think his answer. "Smoke fires help. That, and prayer. A pine branch does less damage to the crop if you hit at the pests. I'll plant apple seedlings and wheat and corn and beans as I have done here. I trap rabbits for Mistress Hardy all the time. Father and Mr. Callahan have taught me to shoot and hunt. I can do a lot." He looked around the long table. "An awful lot."

"Have you taken stock, boy? What do you have? It takes money for supplies. You can't just live off the land. How much do you have?" Mr. Whitman's voice was harsh.

"I have what father put aside for the move. There is his horse, and I'll buy a pack mule." Caleb first looked straight at Mr. Whitman, then directed his attention to the Parson and Mistress Hardy and finally to the others. "I have the generous help you all have given me this day, and I am most grateful." Caleb rose and put his arms about Mistress Hardy, hugging her close. He moved to do this as much out of gratitude as his need to hold onto someone, the need to steady his resolve. Hoping that while he forced his voice to be strong, no one would know he was quivering inside.

"Caleb, what is your age?" This from Daniel Moore, a veteran who had served with Caleb's father in the war. "You're still a boy. What? Thirteen or so?"

"Fifteen, sir. And I'll be sixteen this summer, come July. I'll be sixteen when I reach the Tygart Valley to claim father's acreage."

"Humph," growled Daniel. "Still a boy. Still a boy. No age to be setting off for the frontier. And alone at that. Your father would never approve."

The circle of men agreed.

Suddenly, Caleb felt a presence, as though his father was with him. He continued, "I know to ask for Colonel Humphrey when I get there. Father said he would help us. Father met Colonel Humphrey when his company delivered supplies to the forts in the valley during the war. We were preparing to leave for the mountains but..." and Caleb faltered, at a loss to continue. He tried again. "You see, I, this was his dream and ... " Once again, he could not go on, overcome with the memory of his father.

Mistress Hardy began to gather empty tankards signaling the discussion was over. "It's time to get to work. Caleb, we'll need more wood for the kitchen."

Caleb sighed with relief as the men rose to take their leave. He was grateful for being rescued from the meeting and squeezed Mistress Hardy's hand in thanks as he fled to the woodlot.

After delivering two armloads of wood to the tavern kitchen, Caleb rested for a bit and then returned to cut more wood. He hunkered on a locust stump which he used as his cutting block. He remembered all the comments of the morning and muttered aloud, "Why couldn't I think clearly and answer their questions? I should have told them about learning figures from Pa and all of his careful plans that he told me about and of the goods we've gathered. I'll handle things better the next time." With this thought, he reached for his ax and began to cut more wood.

That night, with the day's work done, Caleb sat quietly beside Mistress Hardy in front of the low burning fire in the tavern kitchen.

She took his hand in hers. "I guess you're set in your mind to go to the mountains and I can't do anything about that but you know you will always have a home here with me. I've not told you this before because your father was planning for the two of you to go west. But, if you stay...that is, if you stay here with me and help me, why, this would all be yours some day. The tavern and everything. It would make you a fine life. I want you to think about it."

"You are so good to me. Always have been. You're my family, you know. With father gone, I have no one else. I owe you so much." Close to tears, Caleb cleared his throat and continued, "What you said about the tavern and all some day being mine, well, that's awful kind of you. But I have to go."

"You don't owe me anything. Not ever. I was never graced with children, and you've been like a son to me. Besides, I promised your mother I'd look after you. You're the son I never had. You're my boy."

"Yes, ma'am," was all that Caleb could manage. After a bit, he took a deep breath and said, "You see I have to. For father and for myself."

The two of them sat a long time, holding each other, until the serving man called for Mistress Hardy from the Tavern's main room. Caleb felt her firm grip on his shoulder as she used him for support to stand. He missed her touch as she started for the door and then stopped, turned to Caleb, and in a sad voice whispered, "God be with you."

Mistress Hardy had arranged for Caleb to journey for a few miles to the crossroads with a tinker who had stopped at the tavern. The ride on the cart through the morning had been a great help on the first day of his journey west. His horse and the pack mule plodded along behind the cart at the end of the rein, which Caleb held first in one hand and then the other as he dangled his feet from atop the goods piled high in the cart.

The steady clop of the horses, the warm, morning sun, the rich scent of ripening fields of corn along the road, all helped lull Caleb in his half asleep musings. The conversation of his father's friends, the memory of his father's sudden illness, his burial, and the kind words and help of Mistress Hardy filled his thoughts. Caleb felt again the gentle touch of his father's hand as he traced the outline of Caleb's face and the playful tug on his forelock. He pictured the shocked look on the parson's face when he finally realized that Caleb was going west and how he almost dropped his Bible. Caleb grinned at the memory. He savored the word, *west*, which brought to mind his imagined picture of the Tygart Valley with its meandering river and ripe fields stretching to the mountains.

Suddenly, with a slowing of the cart, he was jolted into wakefulness by the rasping voice of the driver.

"Well, here we are, my boy. I head down the valley, and you go on to the west."

Climbing down from the cart, Caleb said, "Much obliged for the ride, Sir. You go south, and I ride on to the mountains. My thanks and my wishes for good fortune to you."

"Aye. I'll tell Mistress Hardy when I return that I set you on your way. Good luck to you. God speed."

As the man turned his cart south, snapping the whip over the team, Caleb felt very alone. The morning's musings over the events of the last weeks quickly faded from his mind. While riding in the cart it had been easy to let his thoughts drift, to recall again and again the memory of his father. But now, he knew, he must tend to his journey.

He watched the departing cart until it disappeared around a bend in the road and then pulled at the rein of his horse, "C'mon, Molly. We got a way to go before dark." Molly stood firm. He checked the lead from Molly's saddle to the harness of the pack mule, loosening it a bit. Stepping forward, he turned to give a gentle tug to Molly's rein. Still feeling her resistance, Caleb whispered to Molly, patting her neck and running his hand over her muscled shoulders. "Come on, old girl, we got to get going." He stepped out again, firmly in command. Molly, leading the mule, obediently followed.

"You know," Caleb said, "maybe tomorrow we'll be able to see the mountains."

Isaac and the Widow Duerr

"Mom, I sure wish you'd go with me today. It's gonna be big doin's. All sorts of things to celebrate the start of the war. Polk sure showed old Mexico we're not afraid of them."

Isaac was eighteen and full of energy and with luck, between fighting and selling apples, he'd bring home a little extra money. "All our neighbors will be there. Why practically all of Randolph County."

"Then I'll not be missed. I got garden work to do."

"Please, won't you come? I heard tell there'll be big wigs from Richmond makin' speeches and all."

"I got beans to plant." Elmina's voice was firm.

"The beans can wait till tomorrow."

"The almanac says today. You stay out of devilment and get back here in time to milk."

"Oh, Ma, I'm a man now. I can take care of myself."

"I see how you come back here all banged up. Your granddad Caleb should never have gotten you started fighting."

Issac patiently argued, "I won't get hurt. And it's called boxing."

"I don't want to watch you get beat up. It's enough to nurse your bruises when you get home."

Isaac had been drawn to boxing bouts from the time he attended the one room school on Bickel's Fork. He had missed school even more than most of the students because he was needed to help his mother and granddad Caleb. Hardy, Isaac's father, died from a fever when the boy was ten.

Elmina was a respected healer and mid-wife in the valley but her nursing of Hardy was for naught. Hardy would rally for a bit and then take to his bed, burning with fever and a terrible thirst. Elmina would say after his death, "I know herbs, and I think I used them all and nothing helped. We tried and tried, but we didn't have the right ones."

"Please, Mama. Come with me."

"I said no. I got work. I don't know why you got to fight. Your daddy wouldn't approve one bit."

"I'm telling you I'll be all right. You know every little bit I make boxing is a help."

"We'll not starve. Haven't yet. But you get yourself hurt bad and then what? We argue every Saturday morning about this. But you're bound to go no matter what I say."

"I'll be home in time to milk. Don't you fret, and I sure wish you'd go with me. Folks always ask about you."

Elmina gave him a hard look, then continued with her chore. "Never mind. Just don't get hurt. And don't forget the list I gave you. Now go on if you're going."

His mother turned her head away as Isaac tried to give her quick kiss. It was another effort of hers to show her dislike of his fighting.

Isaac headed out the kitchen door for his horse and was on his way. Two bags with the apples were looped over the saddle horn. He would he joined by Sidney, his neighbor and best friend who lived down river a half mile from the Llewellyn farm. He and Sidney hadn't made the trip for over a month what with spring plowing and planting. But Isaac was caught up with his work, and the day was ahead.

Sidney was waiting for him at the foot of the lane leading to the Matthews' farm. "What kept you?"

"The usual. An argument with Mama. She don't let up on me. Treats me like I'm still a kid."

"Well, let's get goin'. The sooner we get movin', the sooner we get there."

The two boys rode along the Cheat, roiling high along the steep river banks. The spring rains had been heavy and now the forest was bursting with new growth. Sarvis trees in their white clouds of bloom stood out in the canopy of abundant oak and maple that towered over the lower growing thickets of rhododendron and mountain laurel. The narrow lane joined the larger road which led up the steep incline, over Kelly Mountain and then sloped down into the Tygart Valley. There, the little village of Leadsville nestled between Leading Creek and the Tygart River.

The church grounds were in a grove of old oak trees. Here, as on most Saturdays throughout the year, goods were displayed for sale and a busy market was soon crowded as people bargained and traded for needed items. A few farmers had cider for sale and the local tavern of course had hard liquor.

Isaac' set his bags of apples on one of the tables. He had wintered them over in a leaf-filled barrel, and they usually sold quickly. He bought a badly needed new ax head and the goods on his mother's list and stashed them in the church. They would be safe there until he claimed them later in the afternoon. That done, he watered and fed his horse, Job, and turned him to pasture behind the church.

Isaac found Sydney who was watching the horseshoe competition. "Come on, let's go see the dancing." The two boys walked around the church, through the grove of oaks and into the big field where the dancing and, later, the fights would be staged.

The sweet whine of the violins and a banjo's twang greeted the boys as they neared the open field. He stared, wide-eyed, as the dancers reeled about the clearing beside the church. The dance finished and the couples, mostly hand in hand, drifted to the tables set up under the trees. The women of the church were setting out food, each household having provided something. Isaac stepped toward the table, ready for refreshments. It was then he saw her.

His mouth agape, Isaac watched the woman in the pale blue dress as she walked slowly toward the refreshments. He stood, stone still, his eyes riveted to her every move as she slowly reached to untie her bonnet and let it hang by its ribbons down her back. Her auburn hair, freed of its cover, caught beams of sunlight that, here and there, slanted through the leafy canopy of the towering oaks. Isaac was transfixed, enthralled with her every move. To him, it seemed that a special light hovered about her, a prism of colors setting her apart from all the others.

She was quickly surrounded by every man who was single and between the ages of eighteen and fifty. They crowded close, elbowing the man aside who had just danced with her. Those married men who tried to steal a look or edge a tiny bit closer were quickly marched to the refreshment table by their wives who knew a serious threat when they saw one.

Her presence simply added to Isaac's already high pitch of nervousness. It was time for the boxing to begin, and his bout was listed second for the afternoon. The dancing was ended for now but would resume after the boxing was completed.

Sidney, teasing, said, "Close your mouth. You look like you're trying to catch flies with it hanging all open thataway."

"Who is she?" Isaac's voice was hoarse, barely audible.

"You don't know? Where you been, boy? Why she's the Widow Duerr. The Mrs. Sara Jane Duerr now that her husband died and left her his part of that big farm." Sidney laughed and continued. "No use your looking at her, Isaac, she's being courted by every man along the river who ain't married." Sidney moaned a groan of loss and longing, "She sure is something all right."

Isaac led the way to the boxing area, off to the side of the refreshment table. He glanced back over his shoulder, stumbled, and then said, "Oh, yeah. I cut some hay on that farm last August. But I thought she was old."

"Well, I reckon she is, if you figure twenty as old. She's the catch in this valley, that's for sure. Come on now, there's the referee."

Isaac, with Sidney following close behind, joined the other young men who were going to be boxing this afternoon. They gathered around the man who was wearing a bright red shirt.

"Listen young men, I'm Dick Schmidt, the referee. What I say goes. If I say you're out, you're out. You all know the rules. No kicking, no holding, no fingering in the eye. No rings on your fingers, so take 'em off if you got 'em cause I'm going to check every last hand before you step into the ring. All you boxers, get on over here. You gonna fight or flirt? Come on now, get in line. There's four bouts so get in place. You know the doings since I think all of you have boxed before, or you wouldn't be here."

Schmidt walked a few steps away from the group, turned and gestured to the ground at his feet. "Now we got a circle drawn in the dirt over here, and you all know that if you step out of it we call a halt until you step back in. And no hitting the guy who steps out until I give the go ahead. You all got that? Hitting a man when he's looking to step back in the ring, well, that's cheating and if you do it, if you hit a man then, you lose. No ifs, ands, or buts about it. You're done."

There was a low murmur of consent from the men and a bit of a shuffling among them here and there as the time approached for their bouts to begin.

"All right, let's get started. Parson, you want to ring your cow bell there to let folks know we're about to begin?"

Isaac stepped to the side of the ring where he finished unbuttoning his shirt. Granddad Caleb had taught him that a loose sleeve could cost a fight and a shirt gave an opponent a chance for a tight grip to pull you off balance. Unfair as it was, it did happen. A quick, unseen tug on a shirt could throw you and leave you open for a knockout punch. He had not heeded Caleb's advice early on but learned the hard way by losing a bout or two. Now, Isaac handed the neatly folded work shirt to Sidney. "Here, hold this for me, Sid." Isaac stooped to gather a fistful of dirt, rubbing it into his hands, and then slid them across his chest to wipe them free of any excess.

Next, Isaac cinched his belt a notch tighter. This little ritual helped quiet his nerves before a fight. Granddad Caleb had taught him that, too. Isaac could hear his granddad's voice, repeating over and over, "A good tight belt helps you stand tall. And it gives you support to stoop and duck and weave when you have to."

After the first bout ended, Schmidt called out Isaac's name and he stepped to the circle. His opponent was a boy about his own age, a bit shorter and very stout.

Solid as a rock, Isaac thought as he eyed the young man. The one thing which always helped Isaac in all his bouts was his quickness. He was lean, and it was obvious that the boy outweighed him by a considerable amount.

"You sure got a bruiser this time," Sidney whispered.

Schmidt demanded, "Let me see your hands."

Isaac spread his fingers wide to let Schmidt check for a ring or a possible hidden bit of wood or metal squeezed between the knuckles. He felt a trickle of sweat down his neck as his right hand was lifted and Schmidt's loud, high-pitched voice sang out, "Lorn Neely of Leadsville and Isaac Lewellyn of Shaver's Fork. All right, at the signal, do your stuff, boys." Schmidt's whistle pierced the heat of the afternoon, and Isaac was left facing his opponent.

The first few moments the boys slowly maneuvered about the ring with neither of them landing a blow. It was a stand-off, and the crowd began to boo and jeer, urging, "Hit him, hit him." There were cheers of both the boys' names although there were more for Lorn who was a local boy. Isaac, not living in the valley, was less well known but some of the men had seen him box and were rooting for him.

Isaac slowly circled his challenger and suffered the first hit to his left cheek. Lorn was indeed a solid young man, and there was power in his fist which left Isaac with a taste of blood in his mouth. The cut was on the inside of his cheek. Isaac ran his tongue over the wound, then spit, the blood forming a bright, red dot in the dust of the ring.

Isaac heard the cheers of the crowd after Lorn landed the blow. Angry at the crowd, he stung Lorn with a smart belt to his right eye. Isaac figured it hurt because Lorn shook his head and hesitated for a moment. Isaac quickly stepped aside as Lorn lunged toward him. The full swing with his right fist met nothing but air, and Lorn's weight propelled him past Isaac as he received another fast punch of Isaac's to his ear. Lorn lunged again and the two boys ended up in a tight clinch which Schmidt broke apart with a sharp blast of his whistle, sending each boy to opposite sides of the ring.

Isaac gulped in air and exhaled with a hiss, trying to calm himself as Schmidt gave the boys a few moments. The whistle signaled for them to renew their fight. Isaac could see the anger in Lorn's face and in his wild lunges. Isaac, fast and light on his feet, dodged away, each time managing to land another quick blow to Lorn's face. They weren't knock out hits, but each one hurt. Isaac heard the loud cheers from the crowd as he continued to rain smart, biting punches to Lorn's face. He tried to dodge but was caught with a well aimed blow to the side of the head. He reeled from the impact and staggered to engage Lorn in another tight clinch.

Once again, the piercing whistle signaled the fighting to stop. Isaac let himself be pulled away from Lorn and then retreated to the opposite side of the circle. He looked across at his opponent and saw that Lorn was pushing his hands up and over his face during their brief rest.

In this quick glance, Isaac saw the Widow Duerr. She was standing at the front of the crowd, just to the back of Lorn, across the circle. In that quick moment, Isaac was surprised at the widow's flash of a smile at him.

Isaac was so taken aback that his jaw opened in surprise. Dimly he heard the whistle and moved forward to do battle in a daze. She, the Widow Duerr, had just smiled at him. Nothing like that had ever happened to him before, and he was stunned. So much so that Lorn caught him with a straight-armed punch to his chin which set Isaac stumbling backwards across and out of the dusty ring. As he turned to step back into the boxing circle, Isaac caught another glimpse of the Widow Duerr. The bright blue of her dress was like a flower in bloom among all the browns and grays of the crowd. Then the Widow smiled at him again.

Isaac fairly reeled at her quick smile. Trying to regain his balance, he stumbled about in his effort to clear his head and step back into the ring. He felt like he was floating as he again dodged the lunging Lorn. It was as though Isaac could feel the very warmth of the Widow Duerr's smiles. He needed to see them again, and the only way to accomplish that was to clear the ring of his opponent. It had suddenly become more than a game to Isaac. Now he had a goal beyond winning. He darted in close and snapped a quick fist to Lorn's cheek and chin and then spun out of reach of the heavier charges of his opponent. Isaac's fast, stinging punches were taking their toll on Lorn. Seeing his opponent's discomfort and loss of focus, Isaac was finally able to land a very solid hit directly to Lorn's chin. Panting, short of breath, Isaac saw Lorn stagger backward, his arms flailing about to keep his balance as he reeled from the blow. He fell and ended up in a heap at the edge of the ring.

Isaac backed away as he waited for Lorn to rouse himself, but that was not to be. Lorn's face and ear were bleeding and, for him, the fight was over. Isaac reached for Lorn's hand and helped him to stand. Schmidt blew his whistle repeatedly to silence the cheering crowd. After what seemed a long time to Isaac, he heard Schmidt roar out in his high, tenor voice: "The winner, Isaac Llewellyn of Shaver's Fork."

Winded, Isaac moved out of the circle, his eyes searching for a glimpse of the Widow Duerr. He pushed his way slowly away from the fight ring and suddenly she was standing directly in front of him. He was dazzled by her smile as she offered him her handkerchief, softly murmuring, "Here, looks to me like you can use this. Let me wipe your face."

Dumbfounded, he felt the soft touch of the lacy material against his face as she continued, "Your lip is bleeding." Her hand was warm, and Isaac's face felt on fire at her touch.

Isaac took the handkerchief and dabbed it across his mouth as he stared at her. *She's beautiful. And she's talking to me. Me. Isaac Llewellyn.* Isaac was unaware that he had stopped wiping his face and was staring, unmoving, at the Widow Duerr. After a moment, he reached to hand the handkerchief back to her. "This...I mean...Here. Thank you."

"Why don't you keep it for now? Your lip is still bleeding. You can give it back later. I'll be here."

Isaac stood transfixed as the Widow Duerr wiggled her fingers at him as though to shoo him towards the creek to wash his face. He remained speechless as he watched her turn and step toward the picnic tables spread out under the trees behind the church.

Isaac heard, as though at a distance, his name called, "Isaac." He looked around and saw Sidney.

"Come on. Let's go wash up."

"Oh. Yeah," Isaac nodded and allowed Sidney to lead him away.

The cold, clear water of Craven's Run broke the spell that had taken hold of Isaac. Kneeling at the edge of the little stream, drops of water dripping from his chin, Isaac looked up at Sidney. "She smiled at me, you know that?" Isaac's voice was hushed and betrayed his wonderment at this turn of events. "That pretty lady. It sure cheered me on. Doggone." With this last, Isaac slapped his hand into the creek and splashed a spray of water toward Sidney.

"You finally woke up, eh?" Sidney laughed. "Golly be. The whole county is looking to court the Widow Duerr, and she makes eyes at you the first time she sees you."

"She sure is pretty," was all Isaac could manage.

"Talk about luck. You sure got it. But you better wash the blood outta that pretty handkerchief."

Isaac did as Sidney suggested, sloshing the bit of lace in the cool brook. Wringing it out, he spread it carefully on the grass, wiping his hands on his trousers. Isaac looked inquiringly at Sidney. "What can I say to her? I never talked with someone the likes of her before. Not ever."

"I don't know. I guess, maybe, just say thank you and see what she says. Coo, coo, coo." Sidney sprinted back to the churchyard, leaving a trail of taunting laughter in the warm afternoon air.

Isaac snatched up the handkerchief. Clutching it in his hand, he pounded after Sidney.

The boxing was over by the time Isaac returned to the churchyard. Now everyone was gathered at the picnic tables. The women were gossiping as they picked over the array of food, commenting on who might have cooked what dish.

The men, those not busy eating, were paying or collecting the money bet on the bouts. Not all the bets were in coin. Some were for future labor or bargaining the value of work on the roads that were maintained by private citizens. Isaac was all too familiar with the road work.

Each able-bodied male aged sixteen or older could be called into service by a road commissioner in their area. However, if a man owned slaves and two of them worked, the time of the two was counted as one day for the owner, and he was then exempt. So road work was as good as coin to bet or bargain.

Today was also a time for exchanging information, whether about crops, the latest news that had been carried over the mountains, or the buying and selling of tools or horses or livestock.

It was a time for play with games of tag and hide-and-go-seek for the youngsters, while the older boys played ball. For the young girls, it was a chance to show off newly-sewn dresses or a bonnet. Of course it was a time for courtship, too.

When Isaac and Sidney returned after washing up at the creek, they retrieved their tin plates stored in their saddle bags. As Isaac moved along the food-laden table, he looked about for the Widow Duerr, but she was not to be seen. Disappointed, Isaac followed Sidney to a spot under the shade trees to eat their lunch. Finishing, they dipped their plates in the kettle of boiling, soapy suds and again in another kettle of hot, rinsing water.

They put their utensils in their saddle bags that they had stashed in the church. As they left the church to head back into the grove of oaks, Isaac spotted the Widow Duerr. She was stepping off the porch of the minister's house. With a shy grin, he waved at her, then straight-armed Sidney who was teasing him again.

"See you later," Sidney laughed. "Or maybe not if she's got a hold of you." Sidney punched Isaac's shoulder, then quickly dodged away as he scuttled off to join the other young men to pitch horseshoes.

Stepping forward to greet the Widow, Isaac hesitated a moment, then held out the damp handkerchief to her. "It's a little wet 'cause I washed it in the creek."

"Thank you, Isaac." The widow took the handkerchief. "Why don't we get some cold tea and sit for a bit?"

They walked through the grove of trees to the tables of food. Isaac, as though led by a leash, trailed along after the Widow. Then, with their mugs of tea, they made there way to a trimmed log in the grove a little apart from the picnic tables. Isaac, too shy and overwhelmed being this close to the Widow to utter a word, concentrated his attention on the handkerchief which she spread to dry on a stub of a branch. The two of them sat quietly, sipping their tea.

The Widow Duerr finally broke the long silence. "You fought good today. Have you boxed a lot?"

"Well," he cleared his throat, took another sip of tea, and began again. "Yes, Ma'am, quite a few times." He wanted to look at her, but instead he stared into his cup as he swirled it about, watching the tea.

"How did you get started?"

Isaac ventured a quick glance at the Widow, saw that she was gazing at him, and gulped at his tea. It was too hasty a sip, and he choked. Clearing his throat, he recovered his voice and finally muttered, "Well, there was these three brothers in school. They kept beating up on me so my granddad taught me how to fight. He said I had to learn to defend myself and needed to whip their tails."

"And you fought all three of them? That don't seem fair to me, three against one."

Isaac blushed under the Widow's continued stare. His shyness was lessening with the Widow's interest in his fighting. *She really wants to know about me.* But it was the look on her face, the genuine concern that caught his attention. Her eyes were a hazy green, with little glints of brown. The brown was the same shade as the freckles that dotted each of her cheeks, high up under the oval of her eyes. Isaac was fascinated with her freckles and that interest relaxed him as he found his voice.

"I started with the middle one. Caught him alone one day and beat him good. The next day the oldest one challenged me, and I managed to whip him too. Well, I was winning until

Miss Loring, she was our teacher, put a stop to us. Anyway, they didn't bother me no more. And the littlest one? Well, he ran ever time he saw me after that. They're gone now. Their daddy took the family west a couple of years back."

"But how did you get started boxing here and at fairs and all? I heard you do a lot of fighting."

"Well, Mrs. Duerr, you see..." Isaac began.

"...Sarah Jane. Please, call me Sarah Jane."

"That's okay with you? I mean for me to call you personal like?"

"Please. I'm just plain Sarah Jane. I'm sick of Widow Duerr." She gave a little laugh.

Isaac joined in her laughter. "Okay. Anyway, I liked boxing and my granddad helped me. So I started to box every chance I got and, well, here I am."

Sarah Jane nodded at his explanation. Then the two of them once more lapsed into silence.

Again, it was Sarah Jane who at length said, "I was cheering for you to win."

"I thought I saw you smile."

"Yes, and the smile was meant for you. And you know what? I didn't care a bit that folks saw me. Knew that I was encouraging you. Oh, Isaac, I'm so tired of people watching me. Watching and whispering all the time."

Isaac was surprised at her explanation. Surprised and at a total loss as to how to respond.

She continued, " I need someone to talk to. I hope you don't mind. You see, Mr. Duerr died this spring and left me a part of that big farm. His sister and brother want to buy my part, and that's fine with me. Judge Johnston is working on that. He wrote up Mr. Duerr's Will, and he's so kind to me. It's no secret that Mr. Duerr's family didn't want him to marry again. But, oh, Isaac, that's done and over with." Sarah Jane leaned closer as she continued. "The ladies at church tell me to stay home and mind my mourning. And I do that. And hoe corn." Ruefully, she added, "Yes, I do a lot of that, too."

Isaac watched her lips as they formed the words directed to him. Just him. Not anyone else. And her freckles. They were fascinating. He had never seen anyone with freckles like hers, and he wanted to rub his fingers across them to see how they felt against his hands.

There was another long silence between them until Sarah Jane broke it at last. "You came to help harvest last fall for Mr. Duerr. I saw you and asked about you. Mr. Duerr told me you boxed some, and you live over on Cheat with your mother and granddad."

Isaac, deep in the study of her freckles, nodded and mumbled, "Yes, ma'am. I do."

"That's something I don't understand, but maybe you can explain for me. The river is Shaver's Fork but people call it Cheat most of the time. Why is that?"

"Well, you see, it isn't really Cheat River until it meets up with the Black Fork, down at the little village of Parson's. That's about fifteen or so miles north of here. But most people call all the branches of the river Cheat. Easier, I reckon. My granddad says it's always been that way."

"Is it true it's called Cheat because so many men have lost their lives logging along it?"

"My granddad says it's named after a French trapper who was killed by the Indians a way back. But folks think what they will, you know?"

"At least now I have an answer. I've never seen it. The river I mean."

"It's awful pretty. Rough water but real pretty."

"Maybe some day you could show it to me."

"I'd like that. I can come cut hay for you again. I mean, if you need help at harvest."

"Isaac," Sarah Jane's voice was softer, with the slightest hesitation before she continued. "Isaac, you don't have to wait until August to come see me. We could meet here and visit some. That is, if you'd like?"

Isaac was so surprised by her suggestion that he couldn't speak for a moment. He cautiously sipped his tea, finally finding his voice. " Yes, ma'am. You bet. You just tell me when."

"Well, we both got work to do." She reached to touch his arm. "But maybe next Saturday. There'll be market again, if you can get away."

Isaac looked at his arm where she had touched him, as though to reinforce her suggestion. He was lost somewhere between her freckles and the sudden warmth of her hand as he mumbled, "Saturday for sure. I'll be here."

"Good. I'll pack a lunch for us."

"Well," he stammered as he rose to leave, "I'd best get this mug back. You want me to take yours?" Isaac gestured to her mug and spilled what was left of his tea.

"No, thanks. I'll sit a little more until my sister-in-law gets ready to leave. You got a ride ahead for you, so you best git goin'."

"Yes, ma'am. I'll be here next Saturday. You'll see." Isaac stumbled away toward the church to return the mug and get his saddle bags.

It was still hot as Isaac and Sidney rode slowly up and over Kelly Mountain in the homeward trek to their evening chores. Sidney's attempts to tease about the Widow Duerr were met with a threatening glare from Isaac and so they headed for Shaver's Fork without so much as another word between them.

They carefully descended the steep road into the narrow river valley. Here the thick growth of rhododendron lined their way, crowding close to the wagon track that was wide enough to allow Isaac to ride abreast of Sidney. Their horses picked their way along the rocky road that led up river. In the quiet of their ride, the sudden clatter of a stone set rolling by the horse's hoofs, broke the silence now and again.

At last, shattering the stillness, gulping air as though to give strength to his words, Isaac blurted, "What am I gonna do, Sid? She's got me all riled up."

"Well, I reckon if I was you I'd be awful happy."

"Sid, just give me an answer and no fooling around."

"My gosh, you won a terrific fight. Your take was two dollars, and you got the Widow Duerr sitting with you drinking tea. Why I'd be hollering my head off if I was you."

"Sid, she asked me to call her Sarah Jane and to come to see her again next Saturday at the market."

"So? What's the matter with you? You go see her. If you don't, then send me to tell her you ain't coming. I'll be happy to be your messenger."

"It's crazy and I know we just met and all." Isaac's words tumbled quickly one upon the other. "But today, every time she touched me or my hand brushed against her arm or her dress, why I got so excited. Oh, my God, Sidney. Tell me what am I gonna do?"

"You just pick her some wild flowers and go drink some more tea. She sure seems to like you so go get her. I know I would just as sure as can be."

"But what am I gonna tell Ma about next week? She'll start in about how she needs me, and I can't go leaving the farm every Saturday what with work to do and all?"

"You're a big boy. Why, the Widow Duerr's got that farm and money. You'll be set for life. Top of that, she's one good lookin' lady."

"But Ma? What about her?"

"I just told you. You got a life to lead. Besides, the Widow Duerr ain't said 'yes' to gettin' hitched, has she? Don't worry about chickens before they're hatched. Pick her a bunch of flowers and see what happens."

"Ma still treats me like a little kid sometimes."

"Your Ma knows she's got to give you up some time. Listen, you ain't ever gonna do any better than the Widow Duerr. Lessen maybe you go off to Baltimore or somewheres like that and find a princess just a-waitin' for you."

"Darn it, Syd. Don't make fun of me."

"I'm not making fun. I'm happy for you. By this time tomorrow, my ma and the neighbors will be yappin' about what happened between you and the Widow Duerr. You can bet your ma will hear about it. So, you wait and see how she takes it. Come on, it's gettin' late and we got cows to milk. Pa'll be raising the roof if I don't get home soon." Sidney urged his horse into a canter and sped up the long lane to his home.

Isaac waved goodbye to Sidney and rode slowly up the valley. His head was filled with images of the Widow Duerr, her freckles, the way she walked, the warmth of her hand, the way her dress tightened across her bosom when she raised the mug for a sip of tea. That thought brought him to rein in his horse and sit for a moment in silence. His thought was did her freckles, which dotted the deep cleft between her breasts, spill on down her body? And what would it be like to kiss them? Each one of them, one at a time. Isaac realized that he was aroused again the way he had been when the Widow touched his arm. He slapped his face as he muttered, "Get on home, you no-good. You got cows to milk, and they got no freckles." He laughed and hurried on to the chores awaiting him at the farm.

Silently, Elmina watched Isaac as he finished his breakfast. With a brief nod and a cold, "good morning," she had greeted him when he appeared in the kitchen in the early dawn. He wore his new work shirt, and the bright red kerchief knotted about his neck that had been a Christmas gift from her. Now, she sat silent as he dawdled and fussed about.

Finally, breaking the long silence, he spoke up. "I gotta get going. Sidney and his folks will be waiting for me."

"Oh, it's Sidney and his folks, is it? They got a date with the Widow Duerr, too?" Elmina's voice was filled with reprimand as she pushed back her chair and stood, pulling at her apron as she was wont to do when filled with anxiety. Indeed, she had nursed the gossip of the Widow Duerr all week. "Don't pretend you don't know what I'm talking about. Mrs. Perry came by after church the very next day and said the whole valley was talking about how she went after you. The Widow Duerr fixin' to carry off a fine young man to do her work. You think I don't know? Well, I do. So there." Elmina stopped in her anger and frustration. It was a long speech for her.

"We're just meeting at the church market like folks do on Saturday."

"She'll take you away and work you like a mule on that big farm."

"Mother, I'm not going nowhere. Just to the market and eat lunch with Sarah Jane."

"Oh, it's Sarah Jane, is it? What happened to the Widow?"

"She asked me to call her Sarah Jane."

"Mrs. Perry says all that she wants is a man to work for her. Mark my word. Take you away and then what will me and Caleb do without your help? Tell me that, will you?"

"What about me?" Caleb stepped into the kitchen, yawning and rubbing his eyes.

"Mornin', Grandad." Isaac turned back to Elmina. "Oh, Ma, I wouldn't go work that Duerr spread for the life of me. Things gotta be better than them folks let on. All they do is fuss at one another. Why Sidney said everyone knows that Charlene and Hobart Duerr don't like Sara Jane and is treated something awful by them. No, Mother. I belong here on Cheat with you and Granddad."

"If your daddy was here, he'd say the same to you."

"Please, don't fret. I'll be back in plenty of time to milk." Isaac kissed Elmina on the cheek. Then he sped out the door to the barn to saddle Job.

Elmina, her hand raised as though to stop him, muttered, low and barely audible in her disappointment, "Oh, Hardy, I'm gonna lose him. I just know it." She stepped to the doorway and watched until Isaac disappeared down the lane, galloping away on Job.

Isaac rode slowly to Leadsville, following behind Sidney's parents in their wagon. Sidney led the way with their old carriage that they hoped to sell to the highest bidder. Isaac had helped them load it with goods for the auction. Once at the market, it had to be unloaded and the articles placed out for sale. Isaac called to Sidney, "I'll be right back," and rode on past the church and along the creek looking for Sarah Jane.

It was already a hot day, and it was still early morning. Ladies who could afford them held parasols while most men had put aside their jackets and loosened their collars. There was no breeze to stir the long grass about the churchyard and even the huge, old oaks seemed to droop in the July heat. Isaac watched a group of young boys who were jumping in and out of Leading Creek, splashing and ducking one another. Further down stream, toward the river, some men were swimming in a good-sized pool where the creek narrowed and was deeper. Young girls waded along the banks of the creek, squealing in mock horror when sprayed with the splashing of the rowdy boys.

Many of the women were seated along the benches among the tables in the cooler shade of the towering oaks, fanning themselves. They would venture, now and again, to view the assorted wares being offered for sale, all the while dabbing at their face and neck with a handkerchief dampened by sweet water.

Isaac stopped before Sarah Jane who was seated under one of the giant oaks. "I'm sorry I'm late. I'm helping the Matthews today. They're selling their old carriage, and Sidney and me got it full of stuff to auction." Isaac dismounted and flipped the reins over a nearby hitching post.

Sarah Jane smiled at Isaac. A folded parasol and a basket holding the lunch she had prepared for them was beside her. "It's all right. I'm not going anywhere," she laughed. "You go on and help the Matthews. I have our lunch all ready so work up an appetite." Sarah Jane flipped her fingers at Isaac to shoo him on his way.

"Yes, ma'am," was all that Isaac could muster as he led Job away to pasture. To himself, he mumbled, "My gosh, she even laughs pretty."

When Isaac finished helping Sidney, he fetched a little sack from his saddlebag and hurried back to Sarah Jane. He found her waiting in the grove of Oaks. "Here, some hickory nuts I picked for you."

She smiled. "How good of you. Let's walk a little. Maybe down by the creek it might be a bit cooler to eat our lunch. "

"Fine with me." Isaac picked up the basket where Sarah Jane had tucked his bag of hickory nuts and followed as she led the way through the tables toward the creek.

They walked upstream for a bit until Sarah Jane said, "How about resting here?" She paused beneath the weeping branches of an old willow.

"All right." Isaac moved to help her as she pulled a luncheon cloth from the basket and spread it on the grass. Seating herself to one side of the cloth, she tucked her skirts around her legs. Touching the dress, Sarah Jane murmured, "Grass stain. It's the very devil to get washed out."

"That's an awful pretty dress. What will you do if it does get grass stain?"

"Well," Sarah Jane laughed. "The first thing is to hope that it don't get any. But if you do get a stain, then you can work on it gently, oh, so gently, with vinegar and sometimes just a pinch of wood ash." During her explanation she laid out their lunch, carefully unwrapping the cloth-covered sandwiches. "Hope you worked up an appetite."

"Yes, ma'am."

"Of course, all the time you pray that the stain will disappear."

"You really pray for things like that?"

"Oh, I'm teasing you. I shouldn't have said pray, 'cause I don't joke about prayer. It's too important. "

"I'm glad you said that. I pray sometimes. Well, really, I pray a lot I guess. I don't hold with all that screaming in church that goes on with a revival. I just pray quiet like. By myself. "

"I know what you mean about revivals. Not for me, either. I pray, too. My mother taught me when I was way little. She always said, 'Save your prayers for things that are important. Real important.' " Sarah Jane laughed again. "Grass stain isn't one of them."

"Is your mother still in Virginia? Excuse me. I shouldn't ask you personal things."

"You can ask me anything you want, Isaac. That's how we get to know folks. But in answer, no, my mother died when I was twelve."

"I'm sorry, Sarah Jane. I didn't know about her dying." Isaac lifted his sandwich as he continued. "This here ham, it's sugar cured?"

"Yes. Folks around here sugar and salt cure. Back in Virginia, they're more likely to smoke cure."

"Well, it sure is tasty. And the bread too. You're a good cook."

"Thank you. When you're ready, I made us a cake, too. And we have lots of tea."

"It's an awful nice lunch, Sarah Jane. Thank you for asking me."

"Cooking was something my mother taught me. She died when I was a little girl, but she taught me so much. My little brothers were only four then. I want to go see if I can find them some day."

"You think they're in Virginia with your daddy still? Oh, here I go again, asking questions."

"Isaac, I told you that you can ask me anything. I don't really know if they're in Virginia or not. Or where my daddy is. I only heard from him a couple of times in the last few years. And those letters were written by the minister of the church in Barryville. They, the boys, they would be twelve now."

"Six years younger than me," Isaac said. "They do know where you are. Don't they?"

"I don't know. I've been gone four years. I think about them a lot, wondering if they're all right. I know they went to school. At least for a while. But they weren't any good about writing."

"What about your daddy?"

"Isaac..." Sarah Jane hesitated for a moment and then went on. "My daddy, well, I've never told anyone this before. You see...It's hard to tell this. "

"Don't say no more. I don't need to know. You don't have to say nothing."

She leaned closer. "It was after Mother died that he started to drink. He missed her so much, and things just never seemed to go right for him after that. Nothing. Not a single thing. He never was all that strong, and he wasn't any good at hard work. But he could fix things, sharpen tools, too, and that's what he did, mostly. He could tinker with things a bit and then they would be just fine. He even worked on the big mill wheel some. But you can't drink and then try to sharpen tools and fix things. Times were hard, and the harder they got the more he drank. It was awful, Isaac. He tried but he was lost without her." Sarah Jane stopped once more. She took some time before continuing. "I'm talking an awful lot, Isaac. "

"And you go right on talking. I like to hear you."

Then, her voice ever so quiet, she continued. "Isaac, my daddy sold me to Mr. Duerr."

"What? Your daddy sold you? Why you can't sell someone. Well, a slave, yeah, but not one of us. Or maybe you could indenture someone to work for a certain period of time for money or goods or something like that. But he sold you to Mr. Duerr?"

"Mr. Duerr came to Winchester and let it be known that he was willing to pay a good price for a bride since his wife died. He was an old man even then. But girls do get sold. It happened to me. Daddy explained to me that Mr. Duerr was a good man, and he would give me a good life."

"You agreed? To let your daddy sell you?"

"Well, not at first. But I got to thinking about it, and it seemed like a way to help my daddy and the boys. We didn't have anything, hardly, at all. Nothing. Only what little I could grow in a garden. We owed money on the house. The boys had the clothes I could get from the church and make do for them. I was tired of working and trying to make something out of nothing. I met Mr. Duerr, and he seemed awful nice. He told me about the farm here and how he needed a family and all. I could help my little brothers, and Mr. Duerr was so kind. I married him and he brought me here to the valley. But..."

Isaac started to speak, but Sarah Jane placed her fingers across his lips.

"I'm not at all sorry that I gave in to my daddy. I don't hold it against him. Not one bit. Mr. Duerr treated me awful good. But he was too old or I didn't suit him right or something because he was never able to properly, well, he wasn't able to father a child."

"Sarah Jane..." Isaac tried again to interrupt.

"Let me finish. Now Mr. Duerr is gone, and I'm here with you and we're sitting on the grass by Leading Creek. That's what matters. Do you see?" Sarah Jane looked closely at Isaac, searching his face for doubt or dislike of her story of giving in to being sold.

Isaac reached for her hand. It was warm to his touch, and he lifted her fingers to his lips for a gentle kiss. Later, thinking about it, she wasn't sure she remembered how it happened, but his lips found hers. It was a passionate kiss, ending with a tender embrace and Sarah Jane snuggled close within his arms. She knew she had never been so happy as now and hoped he would never, ever let her go.

Stillness hung like a shroud over Elmina's kitchen on this otherwise bright, Sunday morning in August. The long silence was finally broken by Caleb, who cleared his throat, hobbled to the doorway, and spit into the yard. He limped back through the quiet, the scrape of his dragging feet adding to the tense stillness. With a groan, he settled into his chair at the table. Caleb coughed once again and then, his words too loud in the early morning air, spoke up. "Bob Poling told me his two oldest boys are dead set to go join the army. I told him to set them to diggin' potatoes right here if they're so all fired up." Caleb paused, hoping for a comment from Elmina or Isaac. Neither responded. "You know, every fool in the country is gonna be headin' for free land out there in California."

Silence in the the kitchen again. It was so quiet the bawl of a calf could be heard from the barn. It's mournful cry triggered Caleb to plunge ahead. He blurted, loudly and with finality, "Well, I'll give you this much, the Widow Duerr is a right smart looking woman. Yes, sireee. That she is."

Quiet settled once again over the kitchen and the three seated about the table.

The stillness was broken, at last, by the sharp, precise sound of Elmina's knife. She sliced into the fresh baked apple pie, every cut emphasizing her anger. Sliding a piece onto a plate she shoved it across the table toward Isaac. "That's just it. Right in a nut shell. A woman, not a young girl. Isaac, she'll put a ring in your nose and haul you around like a tame bear. You mark my words, young man. She needs you to help her on that farm."

"You've done it again, Mama. A great apple pie." Isaac chewed, his words muffled. "I don't mind a bit being led with a ring through my nose as long as it's Sarah Jane holding the lead."

"Don't try to talk with your mouth full. You know better," Elmina snapped.

"Apple pie sure melts in your mouth, right, Granddad?" Isaac winked at Caleb.

"No good sweet talking me, Isaac. She's two years older, and that's too much for a young man like you. That's my argument, and it's not going to change." Elmina slapped the knife onto the table.

"Elmina, age don't mean nothin' when you're the age of Sarah Jane Duerr and Isaac." Caleb motioned for Elmina to cut him another piece of pie.

"And you're an old fool just like all men when they see a pretty girl."

Caleb chuckled. "There you said it, a girl, not a woman." He laughed at catching Elmina with her own words.

"And some old men can get too smart for their britches." With an angry push, Elmina slid another piece of pie onto Caleb's empty plate. "All she wants is someone to help run that big farm."

Caleb took a bite of the pie, grunted his approval, and followed Isaac's lead. "It's mighty good, Elmina. Sweet, but not too sweet, soft crust, easy on my old gums. Kinda a surprise being made by a woman who's hard as a keg of nails."

"Don't go judging me. I'm not hard. I just see trouble ahead for Isaac, and I'm tryin' to save him that."

"Oh, yes, you are, hard as a rock at times. So much like your Granny Helm. She could outfox the Shawnees, shoot as good as a man, and build a snug chimney. Some women seem to have that knack where a man will build a chimney that'll leak smoke enough to drive you outdoors in a blizzard. Your granny was an old lady when I first crossed the mountains. She was my closest neighbor. Why, she'd bring me a loaf of bread, a hank of sausage or a big hunk of cake when I was batchin' up on the hill in my lean-to those first hard years. She'd come look after me and hold my hand with a touch as gentle as an angel when I was ailing. And you're just like her, Elmina. Cut from the same cloth. Only since Hardy passed, you forget the softness sometimes."

"I miss him something awful." Elmina hesitated. "I try to be guided by what he might do if he was here. To do what's right for Isaac."

"I don't mean to preach at you because I've always been proud you're my daughter-in-law. You did all you could for Hardy. But we lost him. Isaac's a young man now. He knows his own mind."

It was quiet once more in the kitchen. Isaac picked up his plate, rose from his chair, and reached for the other empty dishes on the table. "Here, let me help you, Mama."

"Sit down, Isaac. I can take care of my own kitchen." Elmina took a quick glance at Caleb, and then, a bit softer, continued to Isaac. "It's kind of you to offer, but you do enough and then some." She heaved a deep sigh. "What I can't do is argue my day away with the two of you. All right, Isaac. Ask your Sarah Jane Duerr to come see me for a cup of tea. Make sure you tell her that I invited her and then we'll see." With a clatter, Elmina slid the dishes into a pan to be washed. "Now come on, let's get to the field. I know it's Sunday, but we have late beans to put in. Isaac, I said leave those dishes. I'll tend to my kitchen later. Now, let's go."

Elmina reached for her bonnet and led the way out of the kitchen into the yard and toward the fields.

Sarah Jane let her horse pick and choose its way along the rocky byway that passed for a road on the high bank overlooking the Cheat. It had been two weeks since she had seen Isaac when he extended the invitation to come for tea. Elmina had suggested a Sunday, since even she let up a bit with her work on the Lord's

Day. Sarah Jane looked at the high mountains reaching up along both sides of the roaring river. Bright green rhododendron carpeted the steep hillsides. In places it was so dense, twenty or thirty feet of tangled limbs. She figured it would take a man with a strong ax arm to hack a path through it.

Sarah Jane paused to take in the beauty of the surrounding forest. The sunlight reflected prisms of color where it could reach the noisy, rock-strewn river, while the cleared fields she rode by here and there were a welcome break in the thick undergrowth. Blackberry bushes nodded their branches which bent into her path with their ripening fruit. Grey hawks, riding the valley updrafts, seemed to mark her journey as they drifted in lazy circles over the forest canopy as she spurred her horse forward.

I like it here. Yes, I like it. I could live in this valley along the Cheat. She quickly gave a light slap to her cheek, as she admonished, "Sarah Jane, Isaac hasn't asked you yet. And he might not if this visit with his mother goes anyway but the very best." Holding the thought, she pondered whether this was something that she could ask for help from God. She decided it was important enough and rode on, her lips moving in silent prayer for a good meeting with Elmina.

Sarah Jane looked at the steep slope of the orchard that Isaac had told her would guide her to the Llewellyn homestead. She rode slowly up the narrow lane leading to the house. A wing angled out to the right side of an old cabin which had a long porch extending along its length. Higher up in the wing were two small windows indicating a loft. A stone path led to the kitchen with a sloping roof protecting the entrance. A large barn was off to the left, masked by a towering lilac hedge at the edge of the well-tended flower garden. On either side of the entrance facing the river and the lane, was a bright row of red hollyhocks that appeared to nod a greeting to her.

As she rode past the lilac hedge she called out, "Hello."

Elmina stepped quickly to the kitchen doorway when she heard Sarah Jane's 'Hello.'

Isaac dropped his ax in the woodlot beside a high, long stack of firewood protected from the weather by a bark roof. "You should've let me come fetch you. It's a rough road from Kelly Mountain up the river."

"Oh, Hardy," Elmina murmured, watching Isaac as he hurried to help Sarah Jane dismount. "He is so like you. You stole my heart the first day when I rode here in the wagon with Daddy. That was twenty years ago." Standing quietly in the doorway, she watched the Widow Duerr and her son.

"I was fine. It's beautiful, Isaac. The valley I mean. I kept looking for the big stand of apple trees on the hill like you said. It was easy to see your Granddad Caleb's orchard."

Elmina interrupted from where she stood in the kitchen doorway. "I'm not going to pour tea in the yard. So Isaac, get the young lady on in here where she can sit out of the hot sun."

"Oh, boy," Isaac muttered. Then, with a little cough, he introduced the two women. "Mama, this here's Sarah Jane Duerr and this is my mother, Elmina."

"How do you do, Mrs. Llewellyn. You have awful pretty flowers here."

"Thank you, they're a joy to me. Come on in." Elmina stepped aside, nodding toward the Dutch door.

Once in the kitchen, Sarah Jane handed her a little basket covered with an embroidered cloth. "I brought you this. To go with tea or for later if you want."

"That's right thoughtful of you. What is it?"

"Some ginger nut cookies. Really sweet. That is if I made them right. I used the hickory nuts Isaac brought me."

"Well, sit you down. Here, at the table." Elmina pulled a chair around for Sarah Jane. Then she gave Isaac a little shove toward the doorway. "You get on with your work. You and Caleb can have one of the cookies when you finish up this afternoon."

"What? I thought..."

"...You thought? I bet you did. Mrs. Duerr and I mean to have a get-to-know-you tea, and we don't need you to tell us how. You go on about your wood chopping."

"But...," Isaac hesitated at the doorway. "I mean..."

"You heard me." Elmina spoke softly but firmly as she banned Isaac from her kitchen. Lifting the edge of her apron, she flipped it at him, "Shoo, shoo."

Sarah Jane let out a soft laugh as Isaac raised a limp hand in a goodbye wave to her as he fled back to his woodlot.

"It'll take a few more minutes for the kettle to boil." Elmina hesitated. "I'll just finish getting things ready for supper if you don't mind."

"That's fine with me. Can I help?"

"No need. You just sit right there. I won't be but a minute."

Elmina finished preparing the chicken, placed it in a heavy kettle, banged the lid on and slid the pot onto the hot coals in the fireplace. She rinsed her hands and dried them on a towel. As though delaying the get-to-know-you conversation with Sarah Jane, Elmina took her time as she carefully folded the towel then hung it on a rack beside the fireplace. She pulled a chair back from the table. Seated, her hands tightly clasped together, she placed them on the table between herself and Sarah Jane.

"It's a nice kitchen you have here, Mrs. Llewellyn."

"Why thank you, Mrs. Duerr. It's old. Grandad Caleb built it way back." Elmina lapsed into silence as she noted the neatness of Sarah Jane's dress, the fine leather boots, the store bought bonnet she had taken off and placed beside the little basket on the table. Elmina's fingers ached as she resisted the urge to feel the embroidered butterflies stitched across the scarf covering the basket. She had packed away her embroidery when her little girl died years ago. Put it out of sight, a too painful reminder of what she had lost. The memory flooded her mind. Then it was as though her hand was guided by the memory, moving slowly, against her will, to touch, first with one finger, then another, tracing the outline of the butterflies stitched onto the cover.

Elmina's hand brushed softly across the bright yellow surface of the cloth as she lifted it, sniffing at the basket as she breathed in the sweet aroma of the cookies. "My, your cookies do smell awful good. And this scarf, why it's beautiful." The spicy tang of the ginger cookies and the lovely embroidery had broken her silence. "Did you do this work, Mrs. Duerr?"

"Yes, I did, Mrs. Llewellyn. I've embroidered since I was a little girl. My mother taught me. Of course, then, I didn't have the colored thread I got now."

"I never seen anything this pretty. Why them butterflies look like they might fly away any minute." Elmina lifted the cloth to hold it to her face, feeling the raised pattern pressing softly against her cheek.

"Isaac told me about your flowers and your garden, so I made that for you. I'm real happy you like it."

"You don't mean it? Really? For me? Why, Sarah..." Elmina corrected herself, "I mean Mrs. Duerr. It's just about the prettiest thing I ever saw." Elmina spread the cloth on the table as she smoothed out the fabric, running her fingers over and around the pattern of the two butterflies. "My, oh my. So pretty. I sure do thank you. Why you could get paid for embroidery work like this. You know that?"

"To tell you the truth, I did sell some things and sewed for money. But Mr. Duerr didn't want me doing that, so now I sew for myself. I did make the altar cloth for the church. I had an awful time getting some of those Presbyterian ladies to use it. They said it was too gaudy for an altar. Thankfully, the minister and his wife took my side, so now its on the altar every Sunday. They use it for Vespers, too. I'm right proud of that. It's all angels and flowers, so I don't know what those women didn't like about it. Maybe it was too fancy for them."

"Well, now I have a reason to go to church. To see your altar cloth. And I'll do that on a rainy Sunday when I can't get to the fields. Yes, I'll do just that." Elmina began to fold the scarf into a little square. "So your mama taught you to sew? Isaac tells me you lost her some time ago."

"I was twelve when she passed on. I remember her real well or think I do. Sometimes I think I might make up memories so I'll have them. Silly, but I do that when I'm sewing all by myself and got no one to talk to. So I talk to her."

"That's all right. I talk to Hardy, that's Isaac's daddy, all the time. And he's been gone since Isaac was a little boy. I'm sorry about your mama. Oh, there's the kettle." Elmina hurried to the stove. "How do you like your tea? I have heavy, sweet cream. Almost don't need no sugar if you got that." Elmina poured the tea into two cups she had set on the table earlier.

"Thank you. I'll try the cream."

"Will you have one of your cookies, too?" Elmina pushed the basket across the table.

"Not just yet." Sarah Jane blew gently on her tea, sipped it, then put down her cup, a bright smile curling her lips. "You're right. Don't need any sugar with your cream, Mrs. Llewellyn."

"Mrs. Duerr, Isaac wants us to get acquainted like. He told me about your mama dying and your little brothers. And, well, I don't know how to say this, so I'll just say it. Something about your daddy taking money from Mr. Duerr for you. Isaac wouldn't say no more than that. I knew him to be a good man. Not like the rest of that family. Oh, forgive me. They're your kin folk now. I take back what I said." She moved her cup in little circles on the table top, as though erasing her words.

"Mrs. Llewellyn, you don't have to take nothing back. I don't much care for them, and Mr. Duerr didn't either." Sarah Jane took a deep breath. "About my daddy taking money for me? Well, yes, that's true."

Elmina pulled her chair closer as she reached across the table to take Sarah Jane's hands in hers. "You don't have to say no more. That's all I need to know. My God, that's enough for anyone to know. Selling his own child."

"He, my daddy, he didn't really sell me. He wasn't mean or nothing like that. Daddy just couldn't make a go of it without Mama. He started to drink, and it got a good hold on him. He met Mr. Duerr, found out about his family, who they were, you know, all that. Daddy needed the money for the boys. You see, we didn't have anything. Nothing at all." Sarah Jane shrugged and leaned back in her chair. "He said he made a good bargain."

"Still and all, he took money for you. Of course he's not the first man guilty of that."

"Yes, some money and well, oh, Mrs. Llewellyn, I didn't even tell Isaac this. But my daddy..." Sarah Jane stopped. She pulled her hands from Elmina's and pressed them across her eyes. Then she clasped them tightly together in her lap. "We needed just about everything. We didn't have nothing. Daddy, well...he took a cow as part payment for me. There, now. I've told someone." Sarah Jane's eyes glistened with tears.

"What?" Elmina fell back in her chair as though someone had struck her. "A cow? A cow for his little girl? Why, that's awful."

"I know. I couldn't bring myself to tell Isaac." She buried her face in her hands.

"Here now, here." Elmina moved her chair closer to embrace Sarah Jane. "No need to cry over that. It's said and done." Using the scarf from the cookie basket, Elmina gently wiped the tears streaming down Sarah Jane's face. She took Sarah Jane firmly by the shoulders, her voice strong, commanding. "Now listen to me. No one has to ever know this. You hear me? No one has to know. Not ever, you understand?"

Sarah Jane, finally stopping her crying, blurted out, "If it had been a horse. Not a cow. Oh, a cow is nothing, but a horse. Well it has value and...and..." Tears once again slid down her cheeks.

Elmina continued to gently wipe Sarah Jane's face with the scarf. "Stop crying and listen to me. You helped your daddy and your little brothers. That was a very fine thing to do. This is just between the two of us. If you don't say nothing, God knows I never will. You hear me?"

"Oh, Elmina...I mean Mrs. Llewellyn."

"No more Mrs. Llewellyn. It's Elmina, honey. You call me Elmina, and I'll call you Sarah Jane. All right?"

"Oh, Mrs. Lew...I mean Elmina. You're so kind. But I'd have to tell Isaac. I think he should know."

"Well, that's for you to decide. But, honey, you mark my words. A cow has an awful lot of value. Why it gives milk every day. Every single day. While a horse? A horse can get you somewhere's that's true but only if you're strong enough to ride. No ma'am, a cow is worth a lot, so you just stop fretting over that, all right?"

"A heifer for a heifer." Sarah Jane began to laugh through her tears and repeated, "A heifer for a heifer."

Elmina smiled and then joined in the laughter. "You're a good girl." Then, softly, she continued. "You know something, Sarah Jane? My little girl that I lost, she would be about your age if she'd have lived. Alice Marie, that was her name. You said you talked to your mama sometimes when you're sewing? Well, I pretend lots of times that I'm talking to Alice Marie. Teaching her how to bake bread and all. Yes, I talk to her and Hardy all the time. So don't you go thinking there's bad in your talking to your mama." Elmina began to cry softly as well.

"Oh, Elmina, you're..." Sarah Jane burst into tears again.

The two of them, crying for their losses, sharing their grievances, held onto each other, the tea completely forgotten.

Elmina regained control first. She grasped Sarah Jane's hands and began to laugh.

"What's funny? Why are you laughing?"

"Oh, honey, my baby lamb, forgive me, but well, you see... what you said, a heifer for a heifer..." Elmina broke into a loud, raucous laugh as she pumped Sarah Jane's hands up and down in her explanation. "What if it had been a pig?" Elmina laughed even harder.

"A pig?" Sarah Jane, surprised, paused a moment, then joined in the laughter. "Oink, oink."

"Oink, oink," Elmina, howling in laughter, mimicked her. "You know something," Elmina broke their embrace. "I haven't hugged anyone in an awful long time. Like they say, in a month of Sundays. I think I'll have to do it more often." She stopped laughing, her voice serious. "That is, if you'll let me?"

"Oh, Elmina, all the time. You hear, all the time?" She took Elmina's hands, clasping them close in hers.

Elmina saw Isaac standing in the doorway. "What? What is it?"

"I heard you laughing and wondered what's so funny."

Elmina waved her hand at him. "Never you mind. Get back to your woodlot. I want to show Sarah Jane the house. She's staying for an early supper, then you can take her home."

"I heard you laughing all the way out in the woodlot."

"We're having a very nice visit, so you get on back to your ax. Go." Elmina laughed as she dismissed Isaac with a wave of her hand. "Now git."

"All right. Okay, I'm going." Isaac stumbled out the doorway and into the yard.

"Let me show you the rest of this old house, if you'd like to see it."

"Oh, yes. Please. You have an awful pretty place here along the river."

"Caleb, Isaac's Granddaddy, settled here with a land grant from his daddy after the Revolution. It meant so much to Hardy. There's a trunk in my room that I want to show you. Some things that I made for my Alice Marie. That is, if you'd like."

"I'd love to see them."

"Good." Elmina, holding tight to Sarah Jane's hand, led her out of the kitchen.

It was early evening, the sun just beginning to fall off to the west behind the rolling, endless ridges as Sarah Jane and Isaac rode onto the crest of Kelly Mountain. Isaac reined in his horse as he reached to grasp the bridle of Sarah Jane's mount. "Let me show you the valley from here. There's a rock ledge that gives us a great view." The two of them dismounted, and Isaac slipped the reins of the horses around a low hanging tree branch. He led her across a small clearing onto a rocky ledge that overhung the valley far below. "That's somethin', ain't it?" Isaac gestured toward the valley which the Cheat had cut through ages ago.

"I can see why folks settled over here, even as hard as it is to clear the timber. "

"I'm glad you like it. I love it."

"It was a wonderful tea with your mama. She's not near so hard as everyone says. Did you know she saved all the dresses and things she made for your little sister? They're in a trunk in her room. "

"What?" Isaac was surprised. "You mean for Alice? Why she died a long, long time ago. I was way little then."

"She told me she talks to Alice sometimes, just like I talk to my mother. I do like your mama. A whole lot. "

"Sure am happy that you two got along so well. . . " Isaac stopped and took a deep breath. "You see, Sarah Jane, I want to ask you something. Now that you've met Mama, seen our homestead and all. It's not so grand as the Duerr place. Not near so at all..." Isaac stopped again, at a loss as to how to go on.

"What? What did you want to ask me? "

"You see, I don't have a big farm. There is Caleb's old cabin high up in the orchard above Mama's house." Isaac stopped, as though waiting for Sarah Jane to comment. He was met with silence. In the quiet, one of the horses nickered. "That's old

Job. I named him that because he's so patient. Even when he was a colt."

There was a faint murmur as a rising breeze began to ripple through the thick stand of rhododendron spilling down the hillside below them. In the quiet, Sarah Jane reached to push her bonnet back, its ribbons now bunched beneath her chin. "What did you want to ask me? What?"

Isaac pulled Sarah Jane into his arms, his words tumbling over one another in his excitement. "Oh, Sarah Jane, I know it's only been a couple of months that we've been seeing each other. But I like you something awful. From the time you smiled at me when I was boxing. You were so pretty. I never thought... well, I didn't, you know?" Isaac gently brushed his lips across her forehead. "Oh, I want to kiss every single freckle. Every last one."

"And I want you to. But what did you want to ask me? You haven't said."

"Why, to ask you to marry me. Will you, Sarah Jane? I don't have a lot to offer. Just my part of the farm and some timberland that I've got to clear. "

"Yes. Yes, do you hear me? Yes, I'll marry you."

"You will? Oh, my gosh." He gently moved his fingers across her cheeks and then her lips, every so slowly, tracing the outline of her face as though to prove with his touch she was really there in his arms.

"I saw you when I brought water out to the men last harvest. You were so handsome, and I told you I asked Mr. Duerr who you were." Sarah Jane tilted her face up and pressed her body close against his. "I love you so much."

Suddenly, Isaac took a step back from Sarah Jane and began to pat the pockets of his trousers. In a moment, he held a tiny whalebone thimble out to her. "It's all carved. Scrimshaw. Whale ivory, for you. So's you can show folks I asked you to marry me. I got it from one of the traders a couple of weeks ago. "

Sarah Jane took the little thimble and held it up, tracing the pattern carved on its sides. "Why, it's a ship. A sailing ship. Oh, Isaac, it's beautiful. It's . . ."

"And a star too, you see?" Isaac fairly shouted in his excitement.

"Oh, yes. I see it now. A ship and a star. Oh, my," Sarah Jane turned the thimble about, examining the scrimshaw.

"You really like it? Sidney's mom said that's what I should get you. I asked her cause I didn't want to let on to Mama until you met her."

"It's like the star is leading the ship on its journey. A ship to carry us and a star to brighten our way. It couldn't be more perfect." She clasped the thimble tightly in her hand and hugged him, burying her face against his chest.

Isaac lifted her chin and pulled her closer to him as he gently kissed the tears that spilled down her cheek. "I'm so happy, so God-awful happy. Just wait until I tell Mama and Caleb that you said yes. And Sidney, too. And his mom and dad. And, well just everybody." With that, Isaac let out a great whoop of joy.

Both horses nickered at the loud yell, and Isaac could hear them stamping their feet. "They'll be pulling their reins loose it we don't go." He took her hand to lead her quickly back to the tethered horses. "I got to get you home, or I'll be taking the cows out to pasture by lantern light."

"When we're married, why, I can hold the lantern for you. We won't care how late it is. You best get back. I can get home from here by myself. I'm not helpless."

"I know that. But we've got a bit of time yet." Isaac freed up the reins and helped Sarah Jane to mount her horse. Then, placing both hands on Job's rump, he vaulted onto his saddle. He turned to her with a broad grin. "I feel so darn, doggone good," he laughed as he led her horse onto the road.

They started down the mountain toward the valley floor, riding quietly side by side, holding hands. Isaac slowed their horses again and again to brush his lips across her fingers. At the foot of the mountain, Isaac leaned close and planted a quick kiss on her cheek.

"I better get going. "

"You be careful." She turned her mount onto the road along Isner Creek, raising her hand, holding the little thimble for Isaac to see.

They kept turning to wave to each other until Isaac rode out of sight where the road began to twist upward on Kelly Mountain.

The next Sunday, Sarah Jane walked ahead of Isaac, leading the way along a narrow path on the high bank overlooking Isner Creek.

"This path gets any narrower I won't be able to get Job through all these berry bushes."

"It's just ahead. Right at the end of the Duerr farm. See that big old Chestnut up there? That's where we're heading." Sarah Jane motioned toward the old tree leaning far out over a small pool in the creek.

Now leading Job through the shoulder high berry bushes, Isaac followed her into the small clearing under the sprawling chestnut tree. "How did you ever find this spot? Why you could hide here for a coon's age and nobody would ever know."

"I found it picking berries. Help me." She reached for the basket Isaac had tied around Job's saddle horn. Setting it gently on the ground, she pulled a big kitchen spoon from under the covering cloth. "This is my secret spot, and this is where I want you to help me dig up Mr. Duerr's strongbox."

"Strongbox? Out here?" He stared at her as he looped Job's rein around a low branch of the chestnut tree hanging over them.

"I hid it out here after he died. He showed it to me when we were first married. He said not to let on to Charlene or Hobart that he had a secret hiding place. Well, I understood better after he died. The very evening he passed, Hobart came to my room and demanded Mr. Duerr's gold watch. Charlene was right there behind him and she chimed in, saying, "That was my daddy's watch, so it's family."

"What did you do? Seems to me a widow has the right to her husband's things, family or no."

"That's what Judge Johnston told me when he explained Mr. Duerr's will to me. I didn't tell him about the watch and jewelry. There was a ring and a necklace, and Charlene and Hobart took those too. I figured to go along and not cause any trouble. I knew I'd have enough of that if I was going to stay on in that house." She laughed. "I was sure right about that." She knelt beside an outcropping of limestone that sloped across the grassy glade and down the bank to the creek. She began to dig with the spoon.

"Here, let me do that." Isaac quickly knelt beside her, taking the spoon and digging. "How big is it? The strongbox?"

"It's little. You'll see. I hid it in a basket when I sneaked it out here. I pretended I wanted to be alone and sew along the creek. I did that the day after we buried Mr. Duerr because I was afraid Charlene would search my room and find it."

"I feel something. Is it wood or metal or what?" Isaac probed his fingers into the shallow hole he had dug.

"Leather. Just real thick leather. Have you got it?" She asked, breathless in her excitement.

Isaac pulled a small box the size of a humidor from the hole and brushed the loose dirt from its top and sides. He set it carefully in front of her.

Sarah Jane slipped a long ribbon from around her neck. There was a tiny key in a knot at its end. She cleaned the dirt from the lock and inserted the key. "Oh, it's stuck. It won't turn."

"Here let me try." He tried to turn the key but to no avail. "It's rusted tight." He wiped the key on his trousers and tried again without success. "Being out here in the dirt, it's rusted in just this short time." He sat back on his heels, holding the little key in his fingers.

"Break it," Sarah Jane whispered. "Break it open. It belongs to me. And you, too, now that we're going to be married. Go on. Break it."

He picked up a small stone and pounded at the lock which gave way quickly from the moldy leather. "There you are. Just lift the top."

She opened the slightly rounded leather top and exclaimed, "Oh, my, Isaac. Look. I didn't know there was so much. It didn't seem right to look when he died, but Mr. Duerr must have added to these bills all along. Look. Coins, too. I never saw this many before. Never."

Isaac stared at the bundled bills and loose coins. "Why, looks like there's a whole lot of money."

"I can see that. Count it. I'm too excited. Go on, count it." She pushed the leather box toward him.

He carefully pulled the bundle of bills from the box and began to lay them out one at a time as he counted aloud. As the number passed one hundred, he paused. "I've never seen this much money at one time."

"Go on. Keep counting." Sarah Jane's face reflected the surprise and awe at the riches.

Isaac arranged the bills in little stacks and then did the same with the coins. He carefully counted the orderly heaps, putting his finger on each stack as he touched them. "Two hundred ten dollars in bills. There's another seventy-five dollars in coins. Seven ten dollar gold pieces and one five." He let out a long, low whistle. "Why this is a fortune, Sarah Jane. An awful lot of money."

"Good, we can use it. I'm glad I hid it. It's ours. We can use it to build on to Caleb's old cabin. Why we can make a real good house of it now." She reached to touch his hand. "Oh, I'm so happy that we have this. And there'll be some land settled on me, too, like I told you. Judge Johnston read Mr.

Duerr's will to us the day after the funeral. If I marry, why then I lose any right to the big farm, but the Duerr's have to give me fifty acres."

"Fifty acres. Why, it's. . . ," Isaac was so amazed at this news that he had to stop for a moment to take a deep breath. "All this money and the land, too, why, I can't. . . I can't believe it."

She moved to him, scattering the bills and coins with her skirt. "Elmina told me she still has a bit of a debt on your place. She had to borrow to hire a man when Hardy died because you weren't big enough to take over the workload. We can pay that debt and still have money to build. Oh, Isaac, I didn't know Mr. Duerr had left me all this. I'm so grateful to that kind man. So grateful."

"Sarah Jane," Isaac's voice was commanding as he grasped her hands. "I can't use your money to pay off our debt. That's not right. Folks will be saying I married you for your money. I can't let you do that. No. I can't."

"Who's gonna know? Who? Nobody's gonna know anything unless we tell them. Isaac, I'm happier now than I've ever been in my whole life. It's going to help build our life. Our place. Our family now. Elmina and Caleb will be my family, too. Please understand. Please."

"I don't know. I can make us a good living, and we'd pay off the debt a little at a time. Well, I can. . . "

"Shhh." She put her hand over his lips then knelt over his outstretched legs straddling the piles of money. Isaac was caught off balance as Sarah Jane pushed him backwards onto the grass and moved quickly to sit on his chest. She began to undo the topmost buttons of her dress. "What do I have to do to convince you? What I have, all I have, is yours. We're going to be man and wife. Do you understand what that means. Do you?" She kissed him before he could argue further with her. She kissed him hard, her lips pushing down tight against his mouth.

Startled as Isaac was by her actions, he began to respond, returning her kiss.

She fumbled at the remaining buttons, continuing to kiss him even as she pulled at her dress. "Now, Isaac. Now. Right here on our money and our land. Now." She slipped the dress off her shoulders and down around her waist.

Isaac rolled from under Sarah Jane and reached to help her pull off the dress. He slipped his hands under her chemise and groaned as he began to kiss the freckles on her neck, moving his lips slowly over her shoulders. He pushed up her chemise, lifted it over her head, and tossed it onto the grass. His work shirt was tugged open and followed her chemise. He rolled tightly against her on the disarray of bills and coins scattered beneath them. Murmuring, "Sarah Jane, Sarah Jane," over and over, fulfilling his dream of kissing her freckles one by one.

Homer

It was hot in the loft of the old mill and Homer had been day dreaming, listening to the rush of Cheat River, thinking of a cool swim later in the afternoon in the deep pool a half a mile down river from Bowden. The favored swimming hole in the swift, treacherous Cheat had been gouged out by the rapids in a sharp bend of the river under a jagged rock ledge. On a sweltering day like this, every boy in Bowden would be sneaking away from chores for a dive off the big rock into the always cold Cheat.

Homer had been set to sweeping and cleaning the loft by his father, Talbert, who worked the grindstone below him. Many folks thought him the best miller in the state. But drink having won out, Talbert still worked for his cousin after all these years and had never been able to move his family from the old farmhouse of his wife's grandmother.

High above the floor of the mill, Homer watched as Talbert slipped his hand into his vest pocket, took a a quick glance around, and then sipped from a flask. His dad would be cranky by supper time. July heat and whiskey did that to folks.

Guy, Homer's older brother, was cleaning the sluice. At seventeen, four years older than Homer, he planned to enlist in the Army on his birthday in August. Talbert had promised to sign

Guy's enlistment papers. President Wilson had finally faced the aggression of the U-boats and declared war on Germany that April in 1917, so war was all anyone talked about.

Homer shared Guy's excitement about going off to fight the Kaiser, and he was proud of his brother. Besides, Guy had promised Homer, "I'll send you a German bullet."

Guy's job of cleaning the sluice was cool work while high in the rafters motes of dust and grain drifting in the air settled on Homer's neck and arms, setting him to scratching. His blouse, hanging outside his cotton pants, stuck to his sweaty body. Homer was already as tall as Guy, and he had to stoop and duck under the wide rafters high above the floor of the mill. Dark brown hair, brushy eyebrows shadowing his rich blue eyes, and a ruddy complexion attested to his Welsh heritage.

"Get down here and carry this feed for Mr. Williams," his father called.

Homer jumped and swung down the rafters to the main floor, nodded to Mr. Williams, and lifted the bag of grain onto his shoulder. He stumbled as he hoisted the heavy bag and stubbed his bare foot on a splintered board.

"Darn it," he said as he tumbled over.

The tie on the sack was loose, and the precious feed spilled onto the floor.

"Why you stupid boy," his father growled.

Homer scrambled to his feet, avoiding looking at his father. He knew that spilled grain meant much hard work done for nothing. He dodged away as Talbert grabbed the closest stick and started to cane Homer something proper.

The stick was a rejected scrap, tossed aside, but its jagged edge with splinters was a formidable weapon. The stinging blows cut deep. His father kept on hitting at him even as Homer scrambled across the mill floor to get away.

"Daddy, I'm sorry. I'm sorry."

Mr. Williams, with a sharp edge to his voice, spoke up. "That'll do. He didn't mean to drop that sack."

"No good for nothing. Get up." Talbert kicked at Homer. "Clean up that grain. Get up, I said." Talbert wiped a dirty sleeve across his sweaty face and threw the stick into a corner of the mill.

Homer got up slowly, limping from his bruised foot, bent over from the painful lashes on his legs. Forcing himself to stand straight, he used a shovel and scraped the spilled grain into a small pile. Gingerly, he knelt to gather it up. "Mr Williams, I'm awful sorry. I'll make it up to you. I'll come work for you."

Now at the mill wheel, Talbert grumbled, "Worthless. Just plain worthless."

Homer worked at the spilled grain, carefully gathering it in fistfuls and lifting it into the sack.

"Not much lost, Talbert," Mr. Williams said. "He can work it out in an afternoon. I'll need some help anyway come August. I'll end up paying you, Homer. You've been lucky, Talbert, you got sons and daughters. All I got are girls. Pretty. They are pretty and good to help their mother. And they can work a hay field, but not like Homer can."

Talbert turned his back and opened the flume to start the big mill wheel, muttering more to himself than to Homer or Mr. Williams, "Clumsy, no good."

Homer cleaned up the last of the spilled grain, retied the sack with a double square knot, and heaved it into the waiting wagon. "Tell me when, Mr. Williams, I'll be there."

"You can owe me. I'll need you more come August, haying time."

"I'll work hard," you'll see.

"I know you will. You're a good boy. And aren't you ever going to stop growing? My God, Talbert, he's only thirteen years old, and he's not gonna stop until he tops out over six feet. He'll beat us all."

"Six feet of nothing," Talbert busied himself with the flume and got set to continue his milling. The workday wasn't over yet.

Homer watched as Mr. Williams drove the wagon off toward his farm up the river from Bowden. Still limping, he rubbed his legs and moved to help his father.

Soon, the big bell at the station rang out at five o'clock, tolling the end of another work day.

Talbert stopped milling and yelled to his sons. "You boys get on home to help your ma. You hear me? Don't make me have to come get you." Talbert pulled the big door to the mill closed and fastened the padlock.

"Yes, sir," the boys chorused and dashed off for the eagerly awaited swim.

The cold water stung at first but then helped sooth the raised welts on Homer's legs. The water also stopped the last trickle of blood which had seeped from one of the deeper cuts. They knew their mother counted on them for chores before supper and after a swim across the wide pool and a dive from the rock ledge back into the water, the boys climbed onto the bank under the big willow tree. Using their shirts to dry off, they quickly headed back up the river toward home to help their mother. As usual, they raced, their pants looped about their necks and flapping down their backs. Their wet underwear would dry a bit as they ran. Usually able to keep up or even beat his older brother, Homer lagged far behind. Damn this foot, he thought.

At the farmhouse, Zurah, Homer's mother, was standing on the porch, holding his newborn brother, Marcus. Talbert sat in his rocker, scowling at the world, his right hand holding the flask.

Homer's mother saw him limping and said, "What happened?"

"Nothing, Mama." Homer shot a quick glance at Talbert.

"What do you mean, nothing? I caned him for spilling Mr. Williams' grain all over the floor. He ain't gonna die, so let's get to supper." Talbert stomped his way across the porch and into the house.

"Let me look at them cuts." Zurah knelt and ran her fingers over the raised bruises. "These need a poultice, so fetch me a dozen or so mullein leaves. There's a whole bunch of them growing right back of the garden. Don't pull at them, break them off at the stem. And don't tarry. Supper'll be on the table when you finish up your chores."

After supper, Talbert moved out onto the porch to his rocker and set to cleaning his shotgun. Guy and Homer padded after him, setting out the gun oil and cleaning rags for their father and then hunkered down on the porch floor. Homer winced as he kneeled and settled to sit with his legs stretched out before him.

Talbert scowled at the boys as he wiped the gun. "Don't you kids use this gun no more. It's got a broken trigger guard, and you'll fool around and hurt yourself." The two boys watched in silence. "You leave that fox that's been killin' our chickens to me? You understand?"

They both knew when an answer was expected and mumbled, "Yes, sir, yes, sir." They knew, too, when to keep quiet.

When his father wasn't looking, Homer slipped two gun shells into his pocket.

With the gun cleaning finished and the oil and rags put away, the boys played hide and seek with their little sister, Lillian.

Zurah prepared a poultice of pounded onions and vinegar. Stirring in a few sprigs of mint, she poured the mixture into a bowl to cool. "To fix," she said to Geneva, Homer's older sister.

Geneva, the first born, limped onto the porch. Her feet had not fully formed, and she wore boots to help her walk. The doctor ordered them all the way from Baltimore, and they had cost dearly, as Talbert told everyone, a "pretty penny." Homer fetched her sewing basket and helped her settle onto her sewing stool. She would sew, alongside her mother, until it was too dark to see. There was always mending and, if not, there were shirts and dresses and aprons to sew and quilt squares to fashion. Zurah reminded Geneva, a hint of weariness in her voice, "July won't last forever, nor summer, for that matter. We'll need cover come winter."

As the darkness began to settle around the old farmhouse, Zurah walked into the kitchen and called to Homer. "Let me put the mullein leaves on those welts. Don't pull at them. They'll drop off as the poultice dries. The vinegar may sting a little, but if it hurts that's a sign it's healing. Geneva, watch me so you'll know."

Homer winced as Zurah patted the poultice onto the welts, swollen with abuse from the caning. Her gentle touch offered immediate relief. He heaved a deep sigh as he felt the predicted sting of the vinegar. "Thanks, Mother." Homer scrambled to his feet, the mullein leaves a warm cocoon around his legs.

He didn't know, and Zurah said nothing, but an Old Wives' Tale held that mullein carried magical properties. Zurah knew Preacher Rawlins wouldn't approve if he knew she harbored such methods. "But," she confided to Geneva, "what he don't know won't hurt him none." So she did as she had learned from her grandmother. If the mullein leaves, sometimes called felt wort, helped the healing as well as soothed, then that was all to the good.

When the darkness came and night settled fully about the old house, the kerosene lamps were blown out and the family went to bed, tired from the long day's work and the July heat.

The two oldest boys slept on the porch in the summer instead of in the tiny room over the kitchen–a room warmed in winter by the flue of the wood stove but stifling in summer with no ventilation and its ceiling so low a person couldn't stand upright. Homer liked sleeping on the porch where he could watch the moon and hear the Cheat splashing its way down the valley.

In the quiet Homer lay dead still, waiting, counting minutes. Disobey his father? Use the forbidden gun? If he got the fox that was robbing the chicken house maybe his father wouldn't be so mad at him.

Homer concentrated on the moon as it slipped slowly over Cheat Mountain. He had slept some earlier but now was wide-awake, waiting for the deep night and the moon to rise higher in the sky. He needed the bright light of the moon so he could see his target. The stars seemed so close. He knew they would fade a bit with the moon growing brighter.

Homer recalled asking his father what was beyond the last star. His father had just looked at him for a long time and then went back to cleaning the mill wheel.

When Homer decided the question needed an answer, he asked his mother who said, "You shouldn't ask such things."

"But I want to know."

"Ask your teacher, Miss McDonald. She'll tell you."

Homer would add his questions about the moon and the stars to the growing list he was making. It would be his last year of school, and he had so much to learn. Miss McDonald wanted him to go on in school. "You can commute on the train eight miles into Elkins or board with a family there. You're a bright young man, and you should continue with your education in high school."

"No money for that. Daddy says I'm to work with Uncle Levi on the railroad. I'll start as a water boy, but maybe someday I'll be an engineer."

"You could ask your daddy again. You want me to talk to him for you?"

"It won't do no good. When he says 'no' it means 'no.'"

"I may speak to him anyway. And it's *any* good, not *no* good. You know better."

Guy kicked suddenly and moaned in his sleep. Homer was envious of Guy getting a uniform and journeying halfway around the world to fight the Germans. Well, Homer thought, I can't fight Germans, but if I could get the old fox, Guy would be proud of him. His father, too, and maybe he would stop being so mean.

He studied the moon again. It just seemed to hang there over the porch, casting deep shadows where the old house leaned into the hillside. But he knew it hadn't stopped, was still moving, rising higher in the night sky. Homer wondered if someone was watching it rise as he was now? Another boy somewhere far off in China maybe?

He laughed, remembering Great Uncle Levi telling him he could dig his way there. It had been early one morning when Homer was about five years old when Uncle Levi had stopped at the house on his way to the railroad station. "What you digging for so early in the morning?"

"Worms. I'm goin' fishin'."

"You know if you dig down far enough you'll come out in China."

Homer had stopped digging, intrigued by the thought of China. "Just straight down?"

"Straight down. You can take the fish you catch and eat them with rice when you get there."

Homer had continued to dig, forgetting all about going fishing as he thought of what it would be like in China.

Zurah and Geneva, both carrying hoes, stopped to talk to him. "Homer," Zurah had said, "you ain't ever going to get to China. Uncle Levi was teasing you. Come with Nevie and me if you're so set on digging and let's get at those early potatoes."

Homer trailed after them, dragging his shovel. He was close enough to hear his mother as she said to Geneva, "Uncle Levi is full of devilment. He told me that same story when I was a little girl."

Rolling over to his right side, the better to view the yard and the chicken house from the porch, Homer winced in pain as his leg scraped across the husk pallet. Reaching his right hand to touch the welts that had been raised by the caning, he inhaled the sweet, spicy scent of mint on his moist fingers.

Homer thought of his mother, Zurah. Such a strange name. No one knew where it came from. When asked, she would say, "Mama always said granddad named me. After Granddad died, one of his friends said Zurah might stand for Missouri. The two of them had fought in Missouri during the Civil War and Granddad was wounded there." Zurah would sigh and add, "That's all I know." But she liked her name and was proud of it.

Homer remembered once Talbert had raised his hand to her and yelled "Missouri" as he hit at her. She stopped him, holding up her clenched fists and said, "Don't! Don't! It's Zurah, and if you hit me again I'll kill you. One way or another, I'll kill you." Talbert had just looked at her for a long moment, and then stalked away, out of the house. The children watched, wide-eyed as she thrust her hands towards his retreating back. But whether to push him farther away, fetch him back or retract her hateful threat, Homer would never know. He remembered his mother starting to cry and fleeing the room. That was a long time ago when Homer was a little boy.

Homer wiped the wet from his fingers on the cotton sheath covering the mattress. He could feel the raised threads of the pattern his mother had stitched into the coverlet. She embroidered everything - pillowcases, sheets, dish towels, table covers, her aprons, and all the dresses for the girls.

"It brightens things," she would say, saving pennies to buy the precious yarn. It seemed to Homer that she was always tired now, since March when his new little brother, Marcus, was born.

"One more mouth to feed," Talbert had said.

Homer thought, "Yeah, but whose fault was that?" He knew enough at thirteen to laugh at stork stories and that his own aroused feelings moved him to chase Casey Williams, the pretty neighbor girl from up the river. Casey would flounce about the schoolyard, slip her fingers through her red hair, then shake the loosened curls and slide a saucy look of invitation over her shoulder to Homer. She would do that even when they were in church. Homer liked her a lot.

He had tried to steal a kiss, but she turned away with a laugh. "Get me a buckeye, and I'll let you kiss me."

"A buckeye?" Homer questioned.

"My big sister's boyfriend gave one to her, and she carries it everywhere."

"Where can I get a buckeye?"

"I don't know. Ask. He had to get it somewhere."

Homer wouldn't ask his father. Indeed, Homer had stopped asking him anything. Instead, he asked Great Uncle Levi.

"Oh, sure. There's a big old tree up river a few miles. It's on the Dolly farm along the river. Why you askin'?"

"I'd like to see one."

"It's a nut. Big. The Indians thought the round, lighter eye on them looked like the eye of a buck deer, so that's what they called them. It's supposed to bring you good luck, and I've heard tell that carrying one helps with rheumatism."

Homer and Guy went up river, found the tree, and brought back a handful. They gave some to Zurah, but Homer kept the biggest one and shined it to a fine luster. After church the following week, Homer had caught up with Casey and held out his clenched fist. "I got something for you."

Casey eyed him, suspicious. "What?"

Opening his hand, he displayed the big, shining buckeye. "This. A buckeye. What you wanted."

"Oh, for me?" Casey reached out her hand.

Homer closed his fist. "Gimme a kiss first."

"Here? I can't. If Mama or Daddy sees me, I'll get a lickin'."

"Come down to the river with me." Homer turned and began to slowly walk away.

Casey followed, and at the river, she held out her hand again. "Give it to me."

"Gimme a kiss first."

"Promise you'll give it to me."

"Cross my heart and hope to die." Homer drew his hand over his heart. When Casey closed her eyes, Homer leaned in to kiss her.

After a moment, Casey pushed Homer away and held out her hand. Homer, a bit surprised that he had accomplished his goal, was slower to move.

"Give it to me." Casey grabbed the buckeye from his hand. She gave the shiny nut a quick appraisal, closed it tight in her fist, and raced back toward the church.

Homer stumbled after her, dazed and in ecstasy at his triumph. He could still feel the warmth of her lips. It was his first, real, honest-to-goodness kiss

Under the rising moon, Homer thought, "If I get the old fox Casey might think me a great hunter and let me kiss her again." He grinned at his thought.

Bunching his pants and shirt to his chest, he slipped quietly off the pallet, and crept across the porch. The front door to the house stood open to what sluggish breeze there was. He shrugged his way into his work shirt, leaned against the doorjamb and slipped one bare foot at a time into his pants, easing them over the painful welts. The two shells weighed heavy in his pocket. Slowly, Homer pulled his suspenders up and over his shoulders. So far, so good.

The gun was just inside the door, leaning against the old gun case, right where his father had left it. Homer took a deep breath to quiet himself, for he knew if he woke his father he would get it good. He lifted the gun, ever so slowly, easing it into his arms, turned and crept down the porch steps.

The moon was almost straight overhead and the deep shadows were shortening in its light, growing smaller, shrinking into themselves. The big, twin chestnut trees seemed to form themselves anew and the whole yard was visible where it had been cloaked in darkness just minutes before. Except for the two trees, the yard was clear of shrubbery.

Homer sneaked across the yard to the chicken house built into a low rise of the ground. The back edge of the roof angled down into the hillside, and he could easily hike himself onto it. He carefully leaned the shotgun against the wall and climbed up onto the roof. Then, lying flat on his stomach, he leaned over the edge of the roof and, clutching the barrel end of the shotgun, drew it up beside him. He lay there a moment, breathing slowly. He had done it. Got this far. Now for the fox. He rose to his feet and climbed to the front of the sloping roof. He crouched on the corner nearest the woods and slipped the shells into the chamber. "Now, Mister Fox, you come on," he whispered. "You just try to get yourself a chicken."

It was exciting, lying there and waiting for the old fox to show himself. Homer began to picture his triumph and the excitement of his dad and all the family when he shot the fox. He waited. Homer laid the gun beside him, feeling its barrel and stock against his body and rested, his chin on his folded arms. He watched and waited some more. The air was warm, and there was a gentle breeze. Soon, his eyelids became heavier and heavier, and he fell asleep.

Homer moaned and suddenly awoke with a start. He hadn't meant to sleep. He had been dreaming instead of keeping watch for the fox. The moon was sinking behind Cheat Mountain, and the night would soon begin to fade into day. Stupid he thought. Dumb to fall asleep and miss the fox. Oh, he had hunted foxes during the day. Sometimes in the cornfield where they searched for mice but they mainly hunted at night, especially in the cool stillness just before dawn. And now he had missed his chance.

Then, as though obeying his very thought, the fox appeared at the edge of the forest. It crept slowly out of the cover of the low bushes and trees and paused beside the woodpile. Then it raised its nose to the sky in a slow circle testing for scent. Homer watched, hugging the shotgun. The fox seemed to grow smaller, pulling into itself, and began to slink toward the chicken house, placing each paw daintily into the damp grass, its nose thrust forward, grazing the ground, its tail swinging in a low arc.

Homer waited no longer. He raised the shotgun to his shoulder, took careful aim, and squeezed the trigger. The recoil from the blast banged into his shoulder, but he yelled in triumph as the fox flew straight up in the air, then collapsed in a crumpled heap of fur.

"Got him." Homer laughed and said over and over again. "Got him. Got him."

"What the hell was that?" Talbert bellowed in the early light.

Homer turned quickly and could see his father, pulling on his shirt and hitching up his pants, as he crossed the porch. Barefoot, his shirt flapping as he strode across the yard towards the chicken house, Talbert yelled, "I told you not to use that shotgun."

"I got the fox. Look. I shot the fox."

"I told you not to touch that gun, and I was gonna take care of the fox. Now give it here."

Homer set the stock of the shotgun on the roof. Pleading, he said, "But, Daddy."

"Hand me the gun. Now. You hear me."

Homer lifted the gun by the barrel and leaned over the edge of the roof to hand it down to his father. The unprotected trigger caught on the eave and the second shell exploded into Homer's right arm. He screamed as the pellets tore into his flesh, ripping and tearing his upper arm and shoulder. In agonizing pain, Homer dropped the gun, pitched forward and fell, tumbling head over heels into darkness.

It was black as pitch all around. Not a glimmer of light. Something or someone was holding him down. He felt cold and dampness engulfed him. If he could only find light. Then, from far away, he heard his mother's voice, calling.

"Homer, Homer, you come back here. Now. You hear me? Homer."

He knew that tone, knew she was angry. He tried to move toward her voice. As he did he realized that he must be in the little cave at the swimming hole. He'd have to get into the pool and dive under the rock ledge to come out into the Cheat. That was the wetness he felt. The cave's walls were covered with moisture and the tiny beach was always wet.

His mother called again, louder, "Homer."

He tried to roll into the water, but he felt lopsided. Something was wrong with his right arm. He struggled and slipped into the water, pulling himself under the rock ledge and up toward the faint light on the surface of the river.

Homer emerged into the morning sunlight and discovered that he was lying under a quilt, flat on his back on the grass. He was soaking wet in his own sweat. Then he felt the stabbing spasms of pain and cried out—a long, pleading wail—"Ahhhhhhhhhh."

His mother was holding his face, her grip firm, her hair a tangled dark veil brushing his cheeks. "Homer. Don't you do that to me. Don't you faint again. Look at me. Look at me! You hear me?" Her slaps stung his cheeks. "You hear me?"

Homer tried to move his lips, to answer. Finally, he managed, "Mama. I'm here. I'm here."

"Don't you do that to me. Don't you go away from me again. You stay with me."

Homer welcomed her caresses as Zurah's fingers moved softly over his forehead, brushing back his hair. "Oh, dear God. Thank you. Thank you."

Homer moaned again and tried to sit up. The sun was quickly rising, the night shadows fading, the dew heavy in the yard, on his clothes. His dad stood looking down at him, and Geneva was wrapping his right shoulder and arm with a cloth, tight. So tight it hurt.

"Homer, you listen to me." There was an edge to his mother's voice he had never heard. "You got hurt. With the gun. We're taking you to the hospital in Elkins, on a rail car. I've sent Guy for Uncle Levi. You're hurting some, but you'll be all right. You'll be all right. You hear me?"

Homer tried to sit up again, but his mother's pressure on his shoulders held him firmly on the ground. His right arm hurt something awful, and he was crying now. "Mother?" It was a question, desperate for answers. His memory of killing the fox and then the gun going off into his arm seemed to him to have happened a long time ago. As though a dream. "What happened?" he begged.

"You got shot," Geneva said.

He heard his father, "I told him not to touch that gun."

"Talbert. That's enough. Not now." Zurah spoke in the same voice she had used to Homer. Commanding, forceful, demanding, and completely new to Homer.

"Guy's gone to fetch Uncle Levi and a board," Geneva said, still wrapping his shoulder. "That way we can carry you to the station. It'll be easier for you than trying to walk. So just lie still 'till they get here."

"Neva, I'll finish that," Zurah said. "The bleeding has stopped pretty much. You've got the touch. Just like grandma. Now go get dressed and pack a satchel because you may have to stay. You and your dad can ride with Homer on the rail car."

Through a blur, Homer watched Geneva as she got up, straightening her nightgown. Homer felt her boots brush his legs as she stepped across him. She was the only one of the kids to wear boots year round. Her Baltimore Boots as Talbert called them.

Guy and Homer's Great Uncle Levi arrived with a wide board as Geneva ran to dress. Homer was gently lifted onto the board and carried down the hill and across the bridge to the station house beside the railroad track.

A small crowd had already gathered at the railroad station, the word of the horrible accident spreading quickly through the dusty little village. Miss McDonald, even this early in the day, was already prim in her long skirts and bonnet. As always, she grasped her handkerchief to her bosom, her other hand holding an ever-present book. She moved to Homer and touched his chest, murmuring, "You be a good boy. Get well and hurry back to us." Then she turned to Zurah. "I'm driving my carriage into Elkins this afternoon if you want to go."

"You are so kind but thank you, no. I got too much to look after now I got the baby. Geneva will be there, and she's as good as me, maybe better. But I do thank you."

Miss MacDonald nodded toward Geneva. "She would make a fine teacher. I hated it when your husband pulled her out of school."

"Talbert figured we needed her at home, and I guess we do. With the new baby, I got more than I can handle sometimes."

Hearing her last comment, Levi said, "You do fine, Zurah. Ain't nobody good as you."

"Thank you, Uncle Levi. And thank you for helping. You let me know if they get off and all. I've got to get back to the baby." Zurah leaned over Homer and brushed her lips across his forehead. "Be strong, Homer. Be strong. Make me proud. Nevie will be with you." She turned away with a last tuck to the quilt wrapped around Homer and began to walk quickly toward the bridge across Cheat.

Levi, calm and in command, instructed Talbert, "The dispatcher telegraphed for clearance on the track, and you can leave just as soon as the coal train comes through. A blessing, there won't be a long wait, and Homer will be at the hospital in less than half an hour. Two of my railroad crew, Bud and Jennings, will take you."

The noisy coal train clanked in and hissed to a stop, took on water, whistled its owlish hoot and continued its run up Cheat.

Under Levi's supervision, the hand pumped rail car was rolled onto the track and the two men picked by him climbed aboard. "You look after him now, Talbert." Levi's voice easily carried to Miss MacDonald.

"I told Homer and Guy not to touch that gun. But he wouldn't listen and now, see?"

"Talbert, things happen. It's done, and we can't change that. So you take care of him."

Talbert grunted and climbed onto the rail car, then moved to the front as he nodded to the two men who would be pumping.

Miss MacDonald, holding her handkerchief to mask her lips, whispered to Levi. "What did Zurah ever see in the likes of him?"

"Well, you can't blame her. Talbert was a fine lookin' young man, the handsomest here on Cheat. Too good lookin' for his own good. But drink got him and looks don't change that. Excuse me, Miss MacDonald, gotta help here."

Levi moved quickly and lifted Geneva up and onto the rail car. Then he slipped one arm under Homer's shoulders and the other arm under his legs and with a heave, hoisted him up to lie with his head nestled in Geneva's lap.

The rail car was full with the two men manning the pump, Talbert off to one side and Geneva and Homer on the other. The car was of medium size, about five feet wide and roughly eight feet long. Normally used to transport workers and tools, today it was serving as a rail ambulance and the fastest way to get Homer to the hospital.

Levi watched as the little rail car moved slowly down the track toward Elkins through the morning dampness. Already, the heavy mist was beginning to burn off in the early July heat and fade into the mountains.

Miss MacDoanld broke the silence. "Look. There's Talbert, acting like a commanding general. You'd think he was directing an assault against an army instead of a rail car down the tracks to the hospital. Oh, my, I must watch my tongue. But, truly, I don't like the man."

"Yeah, you're not alone in that. But look there at Geneva. Gentle Geneva. God love her, she is an angel. Sometimes, seems to me, God takes one thing away and gifts you with another. I'm glad Nevie is with Homer. They're as close as a brother and sister can be. Homer's always looking after her."

The two of them continued to watch as the little rail car crept down the track and across the fields through the fading mist along the Cheat.

As the rail car moved down the tracks, Geneva gently wiped Homer's face with a cloth. It gathered speed, bearing the unusual burden through the little village and into the valley toward Kelly Mountain Pass.

Geneva pointed out the bright bloom of the rhododendron and the beginning white of the mountain laurel. "Oh, Homer, see all the deer. They're not afraid at all. They look up as though to say, 'Oh, it's that noisy thing again, and go right back to grazing'."

Homer's lips curled into a bit of a smile, as he winced in pain.

Geneva pressed his left hand. "We're almost to the tunnel. Only a few more minutes and we'll be in Elkins."

There the little car pulled into the rail yard which butted up against the grounds of the hospital. A board was quickly put into use once again and Homer was carried into the lobby of the hospital.

Geneva walked beside him, her hand resting on his chest. She marveled as their little group was quickly surrounded by nurses. One of them knelt beside Homer feeling for his pulse while the others produced a stretcher. Bud and Jennings lifted Homer onto the litter, hoisted it up, and followed the lead of the nurses into a hall of the hospital.

With Homer wheeled away and out of their sight, Geneva stood quietly beside Talbert in the big, vaulted lobby. She reached to touch Talbert's sleeve as she asked. "Daddy, don't you think we should pray?"

Talbert's bitter response cut the lobby's quiet like a knife. "I'm not stoppin' you, am I?"

Geneva felt as though she had been slapped. Hard. So hard that she stumbled to regain her balance.

Homer opened his eyes. He was flat on his back in a bed with a white, iron footboard. It was a room he didn't know with a window looking out at a cloudless sky. He tried to sit up and fell to his side in the bed. Something was wrong with his right arm. Homer lay back into the pillows and moved his left hand slowly to his right side feeling the mattress and the sheets and then a big bandage on his shoulder. And he knew. His right arm was gone. Gone. He remembered the blast of the gun, his mother helping him, the hazy ride to the hospital and lots of strange folks and nurses all in white wearing little caps. Then a suffocating mask was held over his face as he struggled to breathe.

Fully awake now he knew it wasn't going to be the same for him ever again. His arm was gone. But there was something else. It was like he needed to straighten his arm. But he couldn't. His arm wasn't there anymore. He felt for it once more. Nothing. But yet it hurt.

Then he screamed and screamed again, "Somebody, help me. Help me!"

In an instant Geneva was at his side, sitting on the edge of the bed, her arms reaching to hold him. "I'm here. I'm staying with you. I'm here."

"They took my arm. What am I gonna do?"

"The first thing is no more screaming," came a voice he did not recognize.

Homer turned his head toward the door to his room. The strange voice came from the tallest woman he had ever seen in his life. She walked toward the bed and towered over him and Geneva. She seemed to him to fill the room.

She held a small cup. "You're going to take this medicine, and you're going to get better." The big nurse thrust the cup at him, leaned over and supporting him with her arm, pulled him upright in the bed. "Here." She pushed the cup into his hand. "Drink."

"Homer, this is Miss Hankins," Geneva moved off the bed to stand beside the window. "She's the head nurse, and she'll be looking after you."

"Now you're awake, we'll bring you some juice and oatmeal. You must be hungry." When Homer didn't answer, Miss Hankins continued, "Can you talk or you just like to scream?" The big nurse leaned over him, her hands anchored on her broad hips, "Well?"

"Yes, ma'am." He thought, "Mama will skin me alive if I don't talk proper to this lady."

"Good boy. Your sister will be here. If you want anything, you just ring this little bell." She pointed to a small bell on the bed stand.

"Yes, ma'am."

Miss Hankins strode out of the room.

"My God, Nevie, she's one big lady," Homer said.

"She's the very best. She let me sleep in the nurse's dormitory last night, and she's having me do some sewing for her."

A big man dressed in a dark suit with a gold chain across his vest and a black hose of a stethoscope around his neck stepped into the room.

"Homer," Geneva said, "this is Dr. Thompson."

The big man leaned over Homer. "Good afternoon, young man. How are you?"

"Well, I..." Homer struggled to voice how he was feeling.

"That's what I thought. A little groggy, but you're doing fine. You're strong. It took a dose of ether big enough to knock out a mule to put you to sleep." The doctor lifted Homer's left arm and took hold of his wrist. Then he put his hand to his forehead. Next, he pressed the little metal disc of the stethoscope against his chest. "Take deep breaths for me, young man. Deep breaths." Dr. Thompson tucked the stethoscope inside his vest and straightened Homer's hospital gown. "Yeah, you'll do fine. Just fine."

"Doctor," Homer began, hesitated and then blurted. "My arm. I can still feel it. It's all cramped."

Doctor Thompson examined the bulky bandage that covered the stump of Homer's arm. "That'll pass. It's the healing. Now eat. And drink a lot of tea and water." Then, turning to Geneva, he continued. "And you, Missy, your daddy wants you back home, and you do that. You give him this." The doctor handed Geneva a note. "Then I want you back here to be with Homer for a few days as soon as you're able. Your daddy won't give you any trouble when he reads this." He turned to Homer. "If you need anything, send for me or get Nurse Hankins to help you." With a wave to Geneva, he left.

"Oh, Homer, you don't know because you were too little, but Dr. Thompson got me my boots. He's real good."

Homer started to speak but just then another nurse entered with a tray. She placed the tray on the beside table, helped Homer to sit up, and plumped the pillows behind his back. "Eat," she ordered as she set the tray on his lap. The nurse wiggled her fingers at Geneva. "Honey, you call me if you need anything."

When they were alone, Geneva helped Homer put milk and sugar on his oatmeal and watched him eat.

Homer was clumsy as he began to use his left hand to feed himself. "Oh, boy. How am I gonna do this?" He spilled some but continued, slowly and carefully spooning the oatmeal to his mouth.

Geneva wiped his chin. "I'll be back to help you. I'm to stay in the dormitory, and they're paying me to sew. Think of that. Mama will be so happy." She punched her finger at Homer's chest to emphasize each word, "We'll be okay."

Homer put his spoon down and grabbed Geneva's hand. "Yeah, we'll be okay. I'll be okay. But, Nevie, you're gonna have to help me."

Homer finished his oatmeal, and Geneva moved the tray to the table.

"Nevie, something's wrong. My right arm hurts. It's like it's all ... well, bunched up or something. They've got to straighten it out."

"Daddy took your arm to bury. Dr. Thompson gave it to him all wrapped up, and Daddy took it home."

Homer pleaded. "You've got to tell them. They'll believe you. They have to straighten it out. Please. Nevie, it hurts."

Geneva put her arms around Homer. "I believe you. I'll tell the doctor, and I'll tell daddy. You'll be all right. I promise." She held him close, humming softly and caressing his face until he fell asleep.

Two days later, when Geneva got back to the hospital in the afternoon, Homer was sitting on the edge of the bed swinging his feet, out and back, out and back, intently watching every kick. He was wearing shoes and was completely absorbed in watching his feet as he thrust them out and banged them back into the bed.

"Nevie, look. Shoes. Nurse Hankins got them for me. She said I had to have them when I walk about. Do you think they belonged to someone who lost their feet? I mean like I lost my arm? I was afraid to ask her."

"Don't be silly. They have all kinds of clothes here. I've seen them. They're donated by folks. And now look at you. Beautiful shoes. Nurse Hankins told me how well you're doing. Walking all over and in just three days."

"Yeah, and guess what?" Homer said. "I've got a job. I'm going to deliver fresh fruit each day to the men's ward. It's on the other side of the hospital. Doctor Thompson said they talked to Daddy and what I earn will be taken off my bill."

"Homer. What about your arm? Does it still hurt?"

"It did, something awful. But then yesterday afternoon, after my nap, it didn't hurt. I couldn't feel it any more. Oh, the shoulder still hurts, sure, but not my arm."

"I guess you were right."

"About what?"

"I told Mama what you said, about your arm feeling like it needed to be straightened and that it hurt. Well, Mama got Guy to dig up your arm. Then she took water and a cloth and cleaned it. Wiped all the blood off and wrapped it up in a pretty cloth. But first she straightened each of your fingers and pulled it straight, the arm I mean. And then she and Guy re-buried it. She had Guy bring a big rock to put on top of the, uh - well, the grave. So, you know, animals don't get at it."

"Mama and Guy did that? Well, it worked. It doesn't hurt now. Where did they bury it?"

"On the hill, up behind the chicken house."

Homer laughed. "Well, that's where it belongs, I guess."

Later in the week, Miss Hankins led Homer to the men's ward. When she entered the ward she bellowed, "Now look here. Homer is your new delivery boy. He'll be bringing you fresh fruit twice a day and run any errands you might need. You treat him right. If you give him a hard time, I'll dose all of you with castor oil. Hear me?" Smiling at the hoots of laughter that her threat aroused in the men, Miss Hankins took Homer's hand and led him out of the men's ward toward the fruit cellar.

Homer laughed. "They sure do listen to you."

"They better if they know what's good for them. They're a fine group in there. They'll look after you and help you so mind them."

"Yes, ma'am."

Down a few steps, Miss Hankins stopped. "Here we are in the fruit cellars. Everything is sorted out into bushel baskets. The kitchen will give you a list each day for your deliveries."

"Yes, ma'am," Homer answered.

"How are your shoes? You let me know if they start to pinch."

Homer, in awe of this giant angel who was so good to him, quickly answered, "Yes, ma'am. And they're just fine. Thank you."

Twice a day Homer brought fresh fruit to distribute. The men seemed very old to Homer. Most were veterans of the Civil War. Two men were one legged and hobbled about with the aid of crutches and another, who claimed to have known Zurah's grandfather, had lost his left arm. The men reveled in having a young, captive audience in the boy.

One of the men repeatedly argued, "If Lee had not fought a third day at Gettysburg, but had struck north towards Harrisburg, things might have been different."

Another recalled, "Folks ain't likely to forget how it was living under martial law of the Yankees. The damn Yankees took food and anything they wanted at Bowden and Beverly. They robbed along the Cheat and through the mountains."

It was Old Tom, the man who claimed to have known his great-grandfather, who took Homer under his wing. "Now you listen to me young man, you've got a lot to learn. And you, too, young lady. Folks helped me when that damn Yankee doctor took my arm out there in Missouri. I was just a boy then, not much older than you are now. There weren't no hospitals, just the ground and a nip of brandy when they sawed off my arm."

"I was lucky. A kind, older church lady at the camp helped me. Come to find out, she lost her son at Gettysburg. Of course he was a Yankee. Her church got us food and boots and what all. When she saw me, I wasn't doin' so well. Real down in the mouth."

"Well, she fixed that. She fetched her daddy to see me. He sat me down and said, 'Look here' and showed me his hands. Or what was left of them. 'My fingers mostly froze off when I was loggin'. Got lost, wandering around in the snow. My family needed me. Without my being needed, I might have give up. Instead, look at me,' and he swung his arms around and around, as strong as any man. 'I can drive a team, swing an ax, pitch hay and hoe as good as any man. And you, young man, you can do the same. 'Course, you got less to work with than me, but you can still do a lot. You'll see.'" Old Tom stopped to take a pinch of snuff. "I'll help you. Just like I got helped by that fine lady's daddy."

Homer and Geneva were transfixed by Old Tom's tale. Wide eyed by the story, they watched as he bent to untie his boot.

"Now look at me." Old Tom proceeded to quickly fashion a half bow in his shoelace with one hand. "If you can tie a shoe lace, why there's a whole bunch of things that you can handle." Old Tom got up to use the spittoon in the corner of the hall. He walked back to Homer and Geneva and said, "All right, you two, let's get started."

It was an arduous task, and Homer worked at it hour after hour trying to tie his shoes with one hand. Geneva came to sit with him and made a game of it, using different colored ribbons and trying herself to make a bow with one hand. Geneva thought of the many times Homer had helped her. He was always ready to do what was necessary to ease her need to walk, a walk that even with the aid of the Baltimore Boots was awkward and uneven. Maybe now she could repay him. She picked one of the bright ribbons and dutifully tried once again to fashion a single bow with just her right hand. It wasn't easy. "Try tying a red ribbon. I think it's easier if you got a bright color to work with."

"Oh, Nevie, you're crazy." Homer's voice betrayed his gloom as he continued. "How can color help when I fumble around and try to make a bow?"

"A half bow," Geneva reminded him. "Just pretend it's easier with a red ribbon. Make believe. Mama taught me that way back before I got my boots. She told me to pretend I was a princess and was asked to dance by the prince. Helped me a lot to go slow and to walk better. So here. Try this." Geneva handed Homer a red ribbon.

Biting his lip, Homer struggled as he tried to twist his fingers around the ribbon. After hours of trying, he suddenly did it. He had a half bow. True, it was uneven, but it held.

"Whoopee," he yelled. "You're right, Nevie. Color does help."

Geneva beamed at his success and hugged Homer to her. Old Tom gave a loud whistle, signaling the older men in the hall to come join in Homer's triumph.

Old Tom went on and on about the war. He told of the mostly barefoot, half-starved boys who fought through the choking smoke of battle for what some folks now called the *lost cause*. "General Stonewall Jackson was a West Virginia boy, and like me and you, lost an arm. You gotta learn his last words and say 'em back to me. 'Let us cross over the river and rest under the shade of the trees.' If we hadn't lost him, we might have won."

It seemed to Homer that when telling him the stories of the war, Old Tom's cloudy eyes cleared and burned brightly with the memories as though seeing it all again. To Homer, the Civil War became very real. He reasoned that if young men not much older than he could fight in such a war, then maybe he could somehow cope with losing his arm. Old Tom had lived a long and very full life and Homer followed him about, watching his every move. Homer knew he, too, had to learn how to live with just one arm.

Everyone told him he had to go back to school. This was one thing he didn't want to do. He told Geneva, "I can't write with my left hand and if I could how would I hold a slate? No siree, I'm not going back to school. I don't want to be pitied."

Miss McDonald was firm with him when she heard of his refusal. "Like it or not, Homer, you're going to have to learn to write left-handed. If you won't go to school, I'll bring school to you."

She brought him problems to solve about calculating the amount of coal needed to fill a freight car, how many pecks to a bushel of apples, how many board feet in a cord of wood, and the comparative weight and dozens of simple things of measure. Everyday things that he would need to know, things he might have learned in the eighth grade which he had refused to attend.

In early August, Homer got to go home from the hospital. His Uncle Levi spoke with John Calain, a supervisor for the railroad, and Homer was to start as a water boy to the maintenance crews. The first Sunday that he was home, Homer asked Geneva to go with him to the swimming hole on Cheat.

Zurah said, "Take a basket. That apple tree down there ought to be ripe by now. It's always early."

"What's that for?" Geneva pointed to the coil of rope about Homer's shoulders. "You gonna lasso the apples?" Geneva laughed.

"Wait. You'll see." Homer wouldn't say more to her questioning. At the swimming hole, Homer stripped to his underwear and began wrapping the rope about his waist. Looping and tying the other end around a tall chestnut tree on the near bank, he left a play of considerable length in the rope.

Geneva, her curiosity aroused, asked, "Homer, what are you doing?"

"Nevie, I have to see if I can swim with one arm. I've been thinking about this all along in the hospital. You don't have to worry. Just watch me."

"What if you can't?"

"That's what the rope is for. I can't get washed away with the rope tied on to me. You'll see."

Homer waded into the Cheat, which was cold as always. When the water was chest high, he dipped his head under and up, wiped his eyes, and then, taking a deep breath, he pushed off, trying to swim using a side stroke. On the first attempts, flailing wildly with his arm, he sank like a stone. He tried again and again until his movements became more fluid. He learned to hold his body high in the water, stroke with his left arm while making a forceful scissor's kick. The strong kick pushed him forward while he drew his arm back for the next stroke. Homer grew bolder with each attempt, gaining not only in his ability but also in the distance he could swim. He waded back on to the bank and with his face set in determination, untied the rope from around his waist. He glanced up in time to see Geneva's questioning look. "It's okay, Nevie. I can do it."

"I'm scared for you."

"Don't be. I can do it." Homer waded in again and struck off into the river. The strong current carried him a little down stream as his body thrust forward, sinking a bit, then rising again with the next stroke. Slipping at first, Homer struggled to haul himself up on to the rock ledge on the far side. "See, see." He was laughing and hollering like Geneva had not heard him do since before the accident. Standing tall on the ledge, Homer plunged into the river, a deep dive and emerged, breaking the surface, his forceful strokes and kicks propelling him toward Geneva waiting on the bank.

Homer pulled on his clothes, coiling the rope about his chest and over his shoulder. "Nevie, I couldn't have done this without you. You walk with your Baltimore Boots, and I can swim."

"Oh, Homer, you've done so good. We have to tell Mama."

Homer helped Geneva lift the apple basket, sharing the weight of the fruit they had gathered. They hiked through the fields full of tasseled corn and acres and acres of hay awaiting a second cutting. Homer was very quiet as they walked but after a bit, he stopped for a moment, his face very serious, and looked at Geneva across the basket of apples.

"You see, Nevie, this was one of the things that really had me scared. Oh, so did the writing and the learning to tie a half bow and just about everything. But you helped me. So did Old Tom and Nurse Hankins and Miss McDonald. Everyone." Homer hesitated and then continued in a rush. "But I had to prove this to myself–that I could still swim. I kept thinking that if I could swim across the Cheat, then other things would be easier. And they will be. You'll see."

Geneva smiled and leaned over to kiss Homer on his cheek. "I'm so proud of you. Proud of my little brother."

The two of them, older sister, younger brother, continued on along the Cheat toward home, sharing a burden which neither could have borne alone.

The Snyders of Pine Hollow

It was early morning, two days after Germany's invasion of Poland in September,1940. Carver was eating breakfast with his parents when Mr. Albertini called to tell them the Klan had burned a cross at the Snyder cabin.

"What?" John, Carver's dad, yelled into the telephone. The phone was pressed tight against his ear as John continued. "Slow down. Your words are all muddled." Then, his voice tight with anger, he went on. "Why pick on a disabled German who's a United States citizen? No reason to torment that man. Stupid bastards."

The Snyder cabin was on the site of an old logging camp near Pine Hollow where Carver lived with his mom and dad.

Carver felt that he was duty bound to look after Sally Snyder. She was the oldest of the Snyder children and in his sixth grade home room. Sally was new to the school this fall, and her red hair had drawn him like a magnet. That and her spunk. When she was taunted with "You're a German," she would raise her little fists ready to do battle and shout back, "I'm an American. American, just like you."

Carver had bloodied the nose of one of the boys at the bus stop when he taunted Sally, and now no one bothered her. He liked being around her and always tried to sit beside her on the school bus. Carver thought his heart had given a little jump last Thursday on the morning bus ride into school when she had slipped her hand into his jacket pocket. Quick as a flash, he thrust his hand in beside hers and laced their fingers together. Unknown to the other kids on the bus, it was their secret.

Sally's little brother, Lynell, was six and in first grade. He rarely spoke except in answer to a direct question and he was always glancing back over his shoulder, as though on the lookout. It seemed to Carver that he was scared of something, afraid of what might be behind him. The older boys were always teasing him. One day as they waited for the bus, Arch Maddox, a bully, offered Lynelll a piece of candy. When he stretched out his hand, eager for a treat, Arch dropped a dead mouse into his palm. Lynell screamed, and Carver got into a shoving match with Arch. The bus arrived just then, and the driver separated the two boys. They were reported to the school principal by the driver, and both were scolded and given extra home work.

Sally's sister, Clarissa, was in fourth grade and chattered away all the time whether anyone listened to her or not. Her talking drove Carver nuts, but he felt sorry for her. He figured no one else listened to her so he tried. Besides, Sally seemed to like it when he paid attention to Clarissa.

So Carver had become the protector for the three Snyder children. To Lynell, he was a hero. Clarissa adored him because he listened to her, and Sally sometimes let him hold her hand.

At supper that evening, Carver's dad, his voice full of disgust, said, "I thought we were through with all that Klan stuff. We ought to burn a cross at one or two of the Klan's homes. See how they like that."

"Don't talk like that in front of Carver. You know better." Carver's mother, Maxine, as always, protecting him.

"He's old enough to know the Klan is wrong. No reason to bother that man because he's a German. Carver you treat him with respect. He's a fine man."

"Yes, sir."

"One of the women in my Circle at the church said Mildred fell in love with Mr. Snyder when he came through sharpening tools up the Valley." Maxine lowered her voice as though revealing a secret. "She was a Franklin, and they're poor as church mice. Now, she has even less."

"He can't do much. All hunched over he reminds me of a crab. Sharpening knives don't make a body rich. Maxine, we got some things we could have him work on?"

"Sally told me they all saw the men burning the cross," Carver was eager to add more information. "Lynell had gone to the privy and was afraid to come out until his daddy went to fetch him. Mr. Snyder walked them to the bus stop this morning, and he was waiting for them again this evening. Sally told me Lynell didn't want to come to school, but Mr. Snyder made him."

Maxine interrupted, "That's just awful. Children being exposed to violence like that."

Carver continued, proud of his knowledge of the Klan. "Mr. Gilbert, the Algebra teacher, I heard he's Klan."

"Carver, how in the world do you know that?" Maxine's voice went up a full octave in her surprise.

"His daughter, Annie, told Emily Bennett, and Emily told me. I promised not to tell anyone."

"You see that you don't repeat that. You hear?" His dad's voice was firm.

"Yes, Sir." Carver knew when an answer was expected.

His mother nodded at Carver and patted her finger on her lips. "John, we're talking too much in front of Carver. You know, little pitchers have big ears."

"He knows not to say anything." Carver's dad nodded to him. "Don't you?"

"Yes, Sir. Mr. Snyder taught me to tie a butterfly knot. It's hard."

"I hope you said thank you."

"I did. Sally told me her daddy stepped on a mine. He was a colonel. That's almost a general." Carver knew military ranks and uniforms and medals from his Cub Scout manual. "Mr. Albertini said that maybe he and Mr. Snyder faced each other in the trenches during the war."

"I don't know how a man lives with defeat and a wound like he got. For all his crippling, he's strong as an ox. I've seen him heft a hundred pound feed sack like it was a toy."

"Dad, if we get into a war, will you have to go fight?"

"President Roosevelt says we're neutral. I hope we don't get into it."

"I remember so well the day of the Armistice in 1918. The so-called War To End All Wars, and yet here we are again." Maxine leaned across the table and snapped her finger on his ear. "You be nice to Sally but no more fights. You hear?"

"Ouch. That hurt."

"That's why I did it. To remind you of what I said."

The Albertini Grocery served the tiny settlement with basic staples for folks who couldn't get into the A&P in town, a good nine miles or more over Rich Mountain. Carver had started working five days a week after school and a full day on Saturday in the little Italian grocery over a year ago. His beginning salary was seven and a half cents an hour, but this fall Mr. Albertini had doubled his pay. Fifteen cents an hour seemed a princely sum to Carver when so many folks had no job at all during the Great Depression, as it was being called.

"You're a lucky young man to be making this kind of salary. I got paid ten cents an hour if that when I was your age." This speech came from his dad, pretty much on a weekly basis.

Carver's dad had also told him, "Mr. Albertini was gassed in France in 1918. He coughs all year round. That's why he always has a handkerchief in his hand. See you mind him."

"Yes, Sir." Carver snapped a smart salute to his dad.

With his raise, Carver tried to put away fifty cents a week for emergency as his parents had taught him. The coins went into an iron bank his grandmother had given him. It was a tiny replica of a red roofed school house, and Carver kept it stored on the bookshelf in his room where he could see it even when he was in bed.

Mr. Snyder helped unload the big delivery truck that brought goods from Clarksburg once a week. At first, Carver was a bit scared of him. He was a big man. Big all over with a head of salt and pepper hair that always seemed in need of cutting. It framed a craggy face with bushy eyebrows falling over his piercing, pale blue eyes. He crept about, swinging his crooked leg in a gait all his own. Mr. Snyder spoke with a slight English accent, and sometimes he forgot a word. Slowly, as they got to know one another, he would turn to Carver for help who was real proud when asked.

Now and again, Mr. Snyder brought Lynell with him to the store. Those visits became more frequent and slowly Lynell, too, began to work at the store. Mostly, he dusted, swept the porch, and helped Carver shelve the tins of food. Mr. Albertini always rewarded Lynell with a quarter for his afternoon of help. All the while, Lynell followed Carver about like his shadow.

Carver basked in the obvious attention from the younger lad, and they became friends. He trusted Lynell enough to let him play with his treasured collection of arrow heads and John took both boys to scavenge at Rich Mountain, the site of the Civil War battle.

"You know, in three years you can join the Cub Scouts, too." Carver bragged a bit as he continued, "Of course, I'll be a Boy Scout then, but you can have my Cub Scout handkerchief. Why we can even go camping together."

Silently, as always, Lynell continued to follow Carver about as though led on a leash. On occasion, he would grunt or nod in answer, and than glance over his shoulder. It seemed to Carver that Lynell was checking to see if he had been overheard by someone following him.

Snow was threatening; it was bitter cold in mid-December and the little store had sold out of bread. The radio said they were in for a big storm. Right at closing time, Mr. Snyder clumped into the store followed by Sally. She was carrying a bundle wrapped in a feed sack. She had on the cloth coat she wore to school. It was too big for her, and the frayed cuffs were rolled up at the wrists.

"Here, Sally. Put him on the counter for Mr. Albertini."

Sally dutifully hefted the bundle onto the counter.

"What you got there, young lady?" Mr. Albertini had been pulling down the big blind over the front window, getting ready to close. Now he turned back to the counter which ran the width of the little grocery.

Sally pulled aside the sack to reveal a tiny baby. The baby began to cry, and Sally cooed softly and leaned in to kiss him.

Mr. Albertini was stunned. "What? What?" he sputtered.

"It was a hard birth. Mildred was in labor this morning when they burned another cross at the edge of the woods."

"What?" Mr. Albertini was stunned. "Those men burned another cross at your place?"

Sally proudly piped up, "Daddy chased them away with his pistol."

"Hush, Sally." Mr. Snyder pulled Sally close to his side.

Mr. Albertini yelled over his shoulder to his wife, "Katie!"

Carver, wide eyed at the baby, whispered to Sally, "I wondered why you all weren't at school today."

"Take the baby. He'll grow up to help you, like your own son. I can't feed the ones I got let alone another." Mr. Snyder pushed the bundled baby a little closer. "Take him. Maybe...maybe I can have a few things on credit?" He was all choked as he went on. "You know...you know I'm good for it." He leaned against the counter, one hand on Sally's shoulder, the other reaching to pull the sack closer about the baby.

Mrs. Albertini hurried to the counter. "I'm here, Angelo. What?"

"Katie, ring up Doc Grey. Tell him he's got to come out right away and help Mrs. Snyder."

"I got no money for Doctor Grey."

"Don't you worry. We got to look after your Mrs."

"She's awful good. Don't complain but she's poorly."

"Carver, fetch me a baby bottle from dry goods." Mr. Albertini waved his hand toward the back of the store.

Mr. Snyder spoke slowly, as though searching for words, his voice hoarse as he gripped the counter. "Those men, the Klan... they shouted at me, told me to get out." He gestured helplessly, raising his hands in a plea. "We got nowhere to go...nowhere but into the woods."

"Don't you fret. Let me get some milk, fix this little guy some supper." Mr. Albertini pulled a blanket from the shelf back of the counter. "Take this, Sally. It's warmer than that sack." He reached to tap his finger on Mr. Snyder's hand. "You're not going into the woods. We're here to help you."

"Oh, thank you, thank you. I'll pay you back." Then, hovering over the baby, relief reflected in his tone, he proudly continued, "He's got a good set of lungs. I'll give him that."

Sally held her finger to the baby's mouth as she cooed softly and tucked the blanket about him.

"Here, Mr. Albertini." Carver had found a bottle.

Mrs. Albertini interrupted, "Let me have that. I'll get some milk for him. Carver, run get your mom for Mrs. Snyder. Tell her I called Doc Grey, and he's on the way." She hovered over the little bundle and traced her finger gently along the baby's cheek. Her voice, soft, low, she murmured, "You hold on, my little man. I'm gonna get you some supper."

Carver grabbed his jacket and raced out of the store. His house was at the end of the narrow, single street in Pine Hollow while the Snyder cabin was a good walk through the woods.

The next hour or so was busy for Carver. He walked his mother to the Snyders, loaded with a first aid kit, bandages, and a quickly assembled bag of food she gathered in haste. He made three trips back and forth, carrying cans of food and staples from the store while his dad was busy splitting wood for the cook stove, the only source of heat.

As the evening wore on, the little village of Pine Hollow was a beehive of activity. Lanterns bobbed here and there as folks made their way to the Snyder cabin or to Angelo's store. The store was still open because Mrs. Albertini had made a huge kettle of spaghetti. It was for the dozen or so neighbors who were helping in one way or another. Carver, Sally, Lynell, and Clarissa had all gone back to the store to eat.

Two big overhead lights on the porch illuminated Mr. Albertini as he announced in his booming voice that word was to be spread throughout the county. "One more showing of the Ku Klux Klan, and I'll have every Italian in three counties here to help me. Give me a hand to tar and feather every damn Klan member who's not run off to hide in the mountains." This was met with cheers from the folks who were enjoying Mrs. Albertini's spaghetti. The women sat on two long benches along the front wall of the store. The men hunkered down on the edge of the porch.

Carver and Sally were sitting by the steps where they were shielded by the wide eave from the snow which had begun. Carver had his English book beside him.

"My dad says Mr. Albertini is going to announce it tomorrow at the American Legion Hall in town."

"Announce what?" Sally asked.

"What he said. That every Klan member better watch his step. Daddy says you all won't have any more trouble from them."

"I sure hope not. They scared my mama something awful. Me, too."

"Mr. Albertini said he'd tar and feather every last one of them."

"The minister is loaning us the little house back of the church. It's supposed to be for visiting ministers and all, but he said we could have it. Daddy says it has two bedrooms."

"That's great. We'll all help." Carver pointed to the book. "You want to take turns reading the story for English class?"

"Sure. I'm pretty good at English, but algebra is hard. If I'm going to be a doctor I have to learn it. And chemistry." There was a hint of pride in Sally's voice.

"That what you want to be? A doctor like Doc Grey?"

"I think so. Next year we'll get a whole semester of chemistry. I can't wait. Mr. Harmon teaches that, and I hear he's real good."

Carver groaned. "It's required, so I'll have to learn it. History is what I like most. Daddy says I'm to go down to Morgantown to law school. You want to go to Morgantown?"

Sally shrugged. "Right now we can't afford for me to go anywhere."

"There's scholarships."

"Mama says to study hard and keep my grades up and maybe I'll get one."

"You will. I know you will. You're the smartest one in our class."

"Here, you two. A blanket to keep you warm." Mrs. Albertini spread the blanket across their shoulders. "You best get to your lessons." She tapped gently on Sally's shoulder. "Doc Grey wants your little brother home with your mama, so I'm takin' him." She went back into the grocery store as she waved to neighbors returning from the Snyder cabin.

"Thank you, Mrs. Albertini," Sally called after her. She turned back to Carver. "You know your mom has been at our place all evening helping the doctor. She's really great. You must be proud of her."

"Yeah," Carver was pleased of the praise for his mom.

Clarissa, followed by her little brother, came out of the store.

Lynell squeezed in between Sally and Carver, hugging a small bowl of popcorn to his chest.

"Look, it's started." Lynell pointed at the falling snow.

Carver was surprised because, like his dad said, "Lynell was so tight lipped he wouldn't say 'snake' if he stepped on one." Now, happy that Lynell was talking, Carver agreed, "Yeah, it's held off, but now it's starting to really come down."

"If it's a big storm, like they say, we won't have school tomorrow. It'll be on the radio." Sally laughed. "So I won't do my algebra."

Clarissa crept down the steps and lifted her face to the sky, trying to catch snow flakes on her tongue. She wore a brightly knitted scarf and stretched the ends to loop them about her shoulders. "The Church ladies gave me this. Lynell got one too. See?" as she pointed to Lynell.

For now, Carver noticed Clarissa wasn't talking a blue steak. The snow had all her attention. She danced in a circle, arms out stretched, fingers grasping to catch snow flakes.

"You know what?" Lynell asked.

"What?" answered Carver as he took a fistful of Lynell's popcorn.

"We're going to move into a house. Daddy said it has two bedrooms."

“That’s right,” Sally smiled at Carver, she, too, in wonder at Lynell talking so much.

“You wanna start?” Carver opened the reader.

“No, you go ahead.” With that, Sally gently slipped her hand into Carver’s side jacket pocket.

Carver smiled at her, tucking his arm close over the pocket. Using his finger to trace the text, he tilted the book to catch the store’s light, as he began to read. “‘The Ransom of Red Chief,’ by O. Henry. It looked like a good thing: but wait till I tell you. We were down South, in Alabama - Bill Driscoll and myself - when this kidnapping idea struck us. It was—”

Lynell interrupted, “Two bedrooms is a lot, you know? A whole lotta room. And you know what?” Lynell was so excited, his words piled on top of one another.

“What?” Sally and Carver laughed as they answered as one.

Lynell leaned in close as though revealing a deep secret. “We’re gonna keep my new baby brother. And you know what else?” Lynell paused as he gulped down a fistful of popcorn.

“No. What else?” Carver asked. He was happy to see Lynell so talkative and not shying away, no longer afraid.

Proudly, his mouth full of popcorn, Lynell eagerly whispered, “Daddy said his name is Franklin. Like President Roosevelt.”

D-Day

In the early summer of 1944, it seemed as though the war would go on forever. And it was hot. Everyone said it was going to break records in West Virginia. As to the war, I guess most folks thought it would be over in a matter of months when it began in 1939 with the German invasion of Poland. Germany would be slapped down by France and England and peace restored. But all too quickly the Germans were in Paris. Germans in Paris! It was unbelievable. I wasn't the only boy who got depressed on occasion thinking of the future. *The Last Time I Saw Paris* was a big hit in 1940, and one of my joys was listening to Kate Smith sing it on the radio.

When Buckingham Palace was bombed, Queen Elizabeth was quoted as stating, "I'm glad we have been bombed. Now I can look the East End in the face." London's East End had been hit especially hard during the German blitz. My cousin Jean wrote me from Leeds that she, along with many other children, had been evacuated into the countryside to keep them safe from the German air raids.

Since August of 1943, the Army had been staging training maneuvers in the Monongahela National forest in West Virginia. There were tanks parked around the football field at the high school, and a soldiers' lounge was set up in the basement of the Presbyterian Church. Local folks used some of their sugar ration to bake cakes and cookies for the soldiers who were trucked in from maneuvers to enjoy The Canteen, as it was dubbed. Convoys of army trucks rumbled through downtown every day. Like so many cities in the United States, we had a curfew and blackout curtains, and school kids practiced air raid drills. We crawled under our desks with our hands clasped over the backs of our necks until the *all clear* was announced over the school's public address system.

Oh, sure, going off to do battle was patriotic and exciting and the war movies were a must see. And there were the uniforms. Every day we argued back and forth over which was better, the Air Force or the Marines. The Navy was rarely in the running until the rumor spread that for some reason, girls found bell bottoms sexy. And we discovered they also liked that the Navy guys wore a big black tie across their chest.

My buddies and I were twelve years old in the summer of 1944, and we were busy collecting tin foil, newspapers, and magazines as Boy Scouts.

It was extraordinarily hot. My parents somehow found enough money to buy a small, rotating fan from Montgomery Ward. It was so hot crops were wilting in the fields. We had our own well, so every evening I carried buckets of water to our vegetable garden. Dad emptied the buckets into a watering can and sprinkled the rows of plants. We usually kept at it till dark.

I had the longest paper route of all the boys and it ended in Oldfields, a little over a mile from downtown. Oldfields was really only a wide place in the road with an old fashioned country store and a long abandoned, silent gas pump standing nearby. A few houses were clustered along a single, narrow street. Overlooking Oldfields from the very top of the hill was Jordan Wakefield's farm which had been in his family since the Revolutionary War. Jordan and Alice were close friends of my parents; their son, Malcolm, was my brother's best friend.

I later learned that the telegraph office sent a runner to tell Jordan the news where he was working at the mill before dispatching the telegram to the house via a bicycle riding messenger.

When Jordan drove up the hill to the farm, Alice was standing on the high porch that overlooked the steep, pine tree lined driveway and the few houses scattered in the valley below. She was crying and clutched the telegram in one hand and the ripped envelope in the other. Folks said that you could hear her scream all through the tiny hamlet of Oldfields.

Jordan knew Alice needed the comfort of another woman. Who better than her best friend, my mother. The four of them–my mom and dad, Jordan and Alice–were seated at the kitchen table clutching coffee mugs when I got home from my paper route that late afternoon.

When Alice saw me she half rose from her chair, pointed at me and screamed, "You. You're okay and so is your brother." Then Alice reached across the table and attacked Mom, knocking off her glasses and pulling at her hair. Her rasping shout continued, "God gave you two sons, and I have only one. And he's gone. Killed. You have two. It's not fair."

Dad and Jordan pulled Alice back into her chair, and her sudden rage faded into sobbing. She quieted, gasping, gulping air. Her cries became a low litany of "No, no, no."

It was totally unexpected, unreal and scary. I couldn't move. I stood there, frozen in place, her every "No" painful and cutting. I remember trying to figure out what had happened to Malcolm, Buddy's best friend.

Mom retrieved her glasses, brushed her hair back from her face, and quickly moved around the table to embrace Alice. Murmuring soft words of comfort, she somehow quieted Alice and, helping her to rise from the kitchen chair, maneuvered her into the living room. I could hear her quiet, consoling whispers through the open doorway. "He'll be waiting for you." Then something I couldn't understand. More whispers and Mom's strong voice was audible again, "God's house has many mansions." Mom knew her Bible, and she was quoting from it now. That's all I heard because Mom's voice was so quiet again. I guess it helped Alice because I couldn't hear her sobbing any longer.

I stood very still, rigid, rooted to the kitchen floor. My dad motioned me to the table and then to sit.

He put his arm across my shoulders and said, "It's Malcolm. He was killed in the invasion. On D-Day."

Too stunned to answer, I stared. Chubby, bumbling Malcolm was dead? Six years older than me, he was the only older guy I could outrun in our backyard football games. Six years older, he and my brother were classmates and best friends and had graduated the year before from high school. My brother volunteered for the Air Force and was in training as a cadet down south in Alabama. When Malcolm was called up just weeks after my brother left for training, my dad said, "Malcolm will never pass the physical." But Malcolm had passed and joined the other inductees for a group picture in front of the YMCA before boarding the train to Fort Meade in Maryland. This past spring when he was home for a week's leave after basic training, he was trim, agile, and moved with a confidence he had never displayed before.

Laughing, Dad had said to Mom, "Well, I guess it's true. The Army can make a man of you."

I watched Dad as he reached to touch the back of Jordan's hand. Then he turned to me again. "Don't you have some lessons to do?"

"Yes, sir." I nodded, picked up my books, and headed for my room. I mumbled to Jordan as I passed by him, "I'm awful sorry, Mr. Wakefield."

"I know," he patted me on my shoulder.

My room opened on to the living room on the far side of our house, and I quietly pulled the door closed. I could hear the low murmurs of Mom and Alice. Sitting on the bed, I opened my history book and tried to read. The print was blurry, and I realized I was crying. This couldn't be happening. Not here on Oldfields Road. Not to Malcolm. Why he was courting Dorothy Moss, who lived just up the road, and everyone expected them to marry as soon as the war ended and he came home.

I had seen the newsreels of D-Day and knew that we were advancing into France. Things were looking up and every day we made jokes about what we'd do with Hitler and Tojo. And of course we–that is me and my friends–all bragged how we would lie about our ages and enlist and go off to fight for the good old U S of A. That summer, war movies filled our dreams.

Sitting on my bed, the history book open on my lap and unread, I was taken by surprise when my dad tapped on the door and entered. He had changed into work clothes because he'd be helping Jordan with the milking and other evening chores on the farm. "We're going to Jordan and Alice's. There will be folks coming to the farm to offer their condolences and your mother will have to cook and all. Do your chores and make yourself a sandwich. Your mother says there's bacon in the fridge. Then study your lessons. We'll be back late this evening."

I looked up at him and silently nodded. He moved over to me, gently sliding his hand over my shoulders in a quick, easy massage. "Are you okay? You can go with us if you want. It's up to you. You can do your chores later. I'll help you."

I didn't want to be at Malcolm's house with the sadness a death brings. Folks would be whispering and all. I didn't want to be a part of that. "I'm all right. It's just, well, you know. Malcolm..." and I couldn't say any more. I didn't have any idea of what I wanted to say.

"You're sure? You'll be okay?"

"Yes, sir."

My dad ruffled my hair and turned to go. "All right. Eat something and do your lessons. We'll be back late."

After he left, I sat quietly for a while. I needed to do something. What? First the chores. The chickens had to be fed and the feeders cleaned, and fresh straw spread under the roosts. Dad had rigged a sliding chain to the clothes line so Barney, his prize hound, could exercise, running along its length and back again. I had to clean up his mess every evening, then feed and set out fresh water for him.

I finished my chores and headed for my tree house in the woods up the hill behind the house. It was my refuge, where sometimes in good weather I took my school books to do my lessons. I had a board which I spread across my knees as a desk. On that day I took nothing. I wanted to feel the quiet of the woods and the wall of trees pressing close about me, comforting. I wanted to be where I could think without the movie posters lining my bedroom walls reminding me of the war.

Settled into my tree house I thought of my Boy Scout hikes this past winter and Malcolm helping me with my merit badges. He was an Eagle Scout, and I was the youngest scout in our Troop. But Malcolm, even more than my brother, talked the older guys into including me in their project to build a log cabin on Chenoweth Creek. Malcolm had been my other big brother.

Remembering, I looked down through the woods from my tree house. I could hear his voice teaching me how to tie a square knot, over and over until I tied it correctly and with ease. We had played so many times in the woods and in the big barn on Jordan's farm, daring each other to walk the high beams stretching across the wagons pulled in line on the floor below. Again, I was the youngest but I walked the beams, my arms outstretched and patting the air to keep my balance. We dared each other to jump into the forbidden hay mow. Forbidden, because the leap was a good, high jump and landing in hay didn't guarantee not ending up with a broken leg. It seemed that no matter what I thought about, Malcolm was a part of it. Even the meandering Stony Creek which cut through the lower field of the farm where his dad had rigged a tire swing in the big maple tree on the high bank over our swimming hole. Malcolm, with his weight, made a bigger splash than any of us.

I gave up on my tree house as a refuge because I couldn't stop thinking about Malcolm. I headed back through the woods to finish my chores. The chickens had to be penned inside for the night and their water tins refilled. Barney to be taken to his dog house, securely chained and fresh water for him, too. And I had lessons to do for my history class which was the only course I was taking in summer school.

Finishing up the chores outside, I hesitated at the kitchen door. Stepping into the room again made me think of the earlier scene. Alice hitting at my mom and pulling her hair. Her pointing at me and screaming. I had never seen adults weep as they had, all four of them. They were sitting there, around the table, with tears streaming down their cheeks, clutching their coffee mugs. Dad and Jordan, too. Men didn't cry, or so I thought. I slowly entered the kitchen and realized that I wasn't hungry. Maybe a cup of cocoa was all.

While the water heated for the cocoa, I did nibble at a piece of mom's bread which I smothered in peanut butter and her homemade blackberry jam. Her jam was the best. But I didn't make a sandwich or anything. I wasn't that hungry. I took another slice and the cocoa to my room. Since my brother left for the Air Force, I had put most of his things away in the room we had shared.

Dad had helped me as I made it my room. He had said, "Let's keep the big plane hanging from the ceiling. You know I helped him build that one. His first."

But the other balsa wood model planes, along with his air plane pictures, I stored away and replaced with movie posters.

A couple of days later, Dad had asked me, "Where is the aluminum model of Lindberg's *Spirit of St. Louis?*"

I had put under the bed. I pulled it out for him.

"I'd like it to be put on the sideboard in the dining room. That was his Christmas present when he first got interested in airplanes. It has part of one of the wing struts missing, but we'll put that side towards the wall."

It was a good idea. Every time we ate in the dining room, it was like Buddy was with us.

I sat on my bed and opened my history book. I was working on an essay about the Civil War in Randolph County. In that part of West Virginia, folks were still mindful of the war which had ended eighty years before I was born. My great grandfather was a little boy during the last years of the war and had told me stories of the raids by the opposing armies. The Yankees had burned his grandfather Taylor's house twice because he had given hay to the horses of the Confederates.

My goal was to draw a comparison between the war in France and the war of eighty years before right here along Oldfields Road. But thinking about my paper was useless. Trying to draw comparisons between the two wars was hopeless. I kept seeing our kitchen table and my parents and Alice and Jordan. All of them crying. I kept seeing Malcolm.

I finished my bread and the cocoa and closed my history book. Maybe if I slept a bit things would be clearer. This afternoon's happening wasn't at all like the movies. Mom had taken me to see *Cry Havoc*, the movie about the nurses on Bataan. In real life, one of her classmates from nursing school had been in the Philippines. At the end of the movie the nurses decide to stay with the troops to take care of the wounded. Of course they were captured by the Japanese. Mom cried for a week after seeing that movie, and Dad said we shouldn't go any more. Of course Dad only went to Gene Autry movies.

"You just upset yourself. Don't go to those films; they're propaganda."

"I was thinking of poor Ellen."

"Watching that film didn't help her."

Mom thought for a minute and then said, "All right. No more war movies."

Mom's moratorium on seeing war movies didn't last long because *Mrs. Miniver* was scheduled for a rerun in two more weeks. "Don't tell your dad we're going, but I love Greer Garson."

I had missed the first showing because Mom thought I wasn't old enough. This movie was better than *Cry Havoc* because only the young girl and the station master got killed, and Mrs. Miniver captured the German airman who was hiding in her garden after he was shot down. At the end they were all in church as the RAF flew overhead on their way to bomb Germany. You could see the flight of the RAF because about half the roof of the church had been blown up in a raid by the Germans.

When Mom and I were walking home from the matinee she gripped my hand real hard and said, "I'm so glad they let her win the rose competition. You know, little things mean so much. Especially in times like these." Mom cried a little then, too. "And remember," she said as she wiped away her tears, "don't tell your dad."

"No, ma'am. I won't." I didn't say anything to Mom and of course not to Dad, but I thought the shot of the RAF was inspiring.

Mom and Dad were still at Jordan's and the house was so quiet as I tried to go to sleep but there was a big ache where Malcolm had been. I kept picturing his round, smiling face. It was no use. I couldn't sleep. I was wide awake.

I sat up and the first poster to catch my eye on the far wall was *The Fighting Sullivans.* They were all killed in the battle of Guadalcanal when their light cruiser was sunk by a Japanese torpedo. President Roosevelt wrote the family a letter. This had never happened before, five brothers killed at the same time. There had been an issue of their serving together and now, it would never be allowed again. That is, siblings in the same company or squadron or on the same ship.

At supper, just after the news came out about the Sullivan brothers, Dad had said, "You know with all that man has to look after, he still took time to write those poor parents. He is a fine, fine, man." Of course we always listened to Mr. Roosevelt's *Fireside Chats* over the radio. I guess everyone did.

As I tossed and turned in bed, I recalled the end of the *Fighting Sullivans.* The five brothers wave to us, turn, and walk through the clouds of the afterlife.

I was suddenly angry and yelled, "That's not how it's going to be for Malcolm." No one's going to make a movie about him.

I threw the covers off, jumped up, and ripped *The Fighting Sullivans* poster from the wall and tore it in half. Immediately regretting my action, I pushed the two pieces together, trying to match the jagged edges, to make it whole again. Maybe I could tape it. I sat down on my bed and carefully folded the ragged pieces into a small square. I felt like I had hurt the heroic Sullivan brothers by tearing the poster. I whispered to myself as I slipped the poster into my notebook, "I didn't mean to do that, but Malcolm won't be seen by anyone walking into heaven."

Things were all wrong. There was no American flag waving in the breeze for Malcolm and no Kate Smith singing *God Bless America*. There was only his parents and their tears, our kitchen table with the coffee mugs which I remembered I had forgotten to clear away.

I wiped my tears on my sleeve and got up to go clean the table. I washed and dried the mugs and put them in the cupboard. Then I wiped the table and sat down in my dad's chair. My dad's and mom's chairs were from the old farm at Bowden, but the table and benches along its sides had been newly fashioned by Great Uncle Bob using curly maple. They reminded me of my cousin Stub, Uncle Bob's youngest son. He had left at the same time as Malcolm but he shipped out from San Francisco and now was somewhere in the Pacific. I smoothed my hands over the beautiful wood of the table top, thinking, *They left together, and Malcolm was killed on D-Day. What if Stub was to be killed too?*

Sitting there, it seemed to me I could still hear Alice's *No, no, no.* Hunched over the kitchen table, I continued to trace the pattern in the wood with my index finger, over and over as I started to cry.

Dad and Mom woke me up when they returned late in the evening from Jordan's and Alice's.

Mom cried out, "Are you all right? What's wrong? Why aren't you in bed?" Her questions tumbling out one after another.

Dad was slower to speak but then, quietly, he said, "Hey, old buddy. Let's get you to bed. You've got summer school tomorrow."

Mom said, "I'm going to turn down your bed."

After Mom left, Dad helped me up from the table. I went to the bathroom and when I walked into my bedroom, Dad had set the fan in the doorway.

"It will help circulate the air better there. It's so dang hot. Gonna be a record if this heat keeps on. I hate to even close the doors. I'll turn out the lights on the porch and in the kitchen and be right back."

Mom came into my room. She was dressed in her nightgown and carrying her housecoat which she placed over the chair beside my bed. She crawled into my bed and nestled up along the wall. Pulling a pillow into her lap and against her chest, she rested her chin in its softness. For a moment I thought she looked like a little girl at a sleepover.

"Lots of folks asked about you tonight. I think everyone in Oldfields was there and half of Newtown. Of course you deliver their papers, and they see you most days." Then she started in about my studies. "Have you finished your lesson for tomorrow?"

I lied when I mumbled, "Yes, ma'am."

Dad came in and switched off the ceiling light but left the little table lamp next to the bed on. He sat beside me on the bed, slipped off his shoes, loosened his belt and, still wearing his work clothes, stretched out beside me on top of the cover. There I was, sandwiched between my mom and dad.

"How is your essay going?" Dad asked.

"I can't get started on it. I don't know what to say."

"Write about Malcolm. I know it's hard, his dying, our losing him, but it's like your Uncle Ray getting shot in the Civil War. Folks get killed in wars. Write about Uncle Ray and the stories Granddad told you. Think about it. Write about people you know. You'll do fine."

I mumbled, "Thank you," but it was easier said than done. I thought about Granddad. I called him granddad although he was my great grandfather. Dad said many times, "Granddad was an old man when I was a little boy, and he's still going strong."

Dad began to talk across me to Mom in the dim light. His voice was quiet, soft, not a whisper, but not loud. "There were so many cars they couldn't get up the drive anymore. We had them park on the road at the bottom of the hill and even across the bridge into Oldfields"

"I am so worried about Alice," Mom said.

"Jordan's sister and brother-in-law drove over from Hillsdale, and they're going to stay for a while. They'll be a comfort for Alice, and Jordan can always use an extra hand on the farm." Dad chuckled. "Jordan's building another shed. Like he needs one more. At least it'll keep his mind and hands busy."

"She turned on me," Mom's voice choked. "I know she's hurting. It was so awful. I hadn't thought she'd attack me."

Dad reached across me and grasped her hand. "Now, now. That was shock. She didn't mean to hurt you. I'm glad we were here to help get them through the first of their grief." Then he turned to me, "You all right?" Before I could answer he continued, "Go to sleep. You've got school tomorrow and your paper route." There was a bit of a sharp edge to his voice, not scolding really, but a little upsetting to hear.

I murmured, "I'm okay." In truth, I was kinda drifting, half way asleep. I didn't think it strange any longer that my mom and dad were here in bed with me. I liked them there and was glad I didn't have to talk much. Their voices continued, half whispers, speculating about how Jordan and Alice would be. About memories of Malcolm.

Finally, I dared to say what I had been thinking. That big "what if…". I forced the words out. "What about Bud? What if something happens to him?"

"Now, don't fret," Dad said. "Bud's in training and things are looking good for the Allies. He may never have to go overseas." Then, more quietly, he added, "We don't cross bridges before we get to them. We'll do fine. Just fine." My dad's voice was consoling and reassuring in the heat of the summer night.

I was glad his voice had lost the edge it had earlier.

I don't remember my mom's answer. Or even if there was one. I was comfortable there, snuggled between them. Every so often I felt the caressing breeze from the fan, brushing across the three of us as I drifted in and out of the edges of sleep. Malcolm had looked so good in his uniform, and I thought about Dorothy Moss just up the road.

Suddenly, I sat up and blurted, "Were Malcolm and Dorothy engaged?"

"I thought you were asleep," Mom scolded. "No, they weren't actually engaged, but Dorothy told me they talked about going down to Morgantown after they were married. She wants to study nursing and Malcolm was set on law school."

"Oh," was all I could muster. But it was as though my mind finally had been unlocked, and I remembered the big sign in front of the courthouse with all the names of the soldiers serving from the county. And of how Mom had cut out the picture of all the draftees photographed in front of the YMCA on their day of departure for Fort Meade in far off Maryland. It had taken half a page of the newspaper. She pasted it into her album.

I thought about the information that was slowly coming out about the horrors of the Holocaust and the heroic feats of the French Underground. And I pictured the Yankees burning the Taylor farmhouse at Bowden.

"Where is the old Taylor house at Bowden?" I asked. "I can't remember."

"That's because you never saw it. Old Mr. Taylor refused to rebuild after the Yankees burned it the second time. I think he moved in with one of his daughters. Why aren't you asleep?" Dad's voice was gruff.

I knew they wanted me to fall asleep but my mind was reeling. "I'm remembering all the things Granddad told me. About the men sleeping in the woods with their horses and cattle to keep them hidden from both the armies. And about Great-Great Uncle Ray who the Yankees tried to arrest as a hostage. I read the Yankees sent thirteen area men who were working on the road to Fort Delaware near Philadelphia as hostages. Only four survived."

"That sounds right," Dad said.

"Granddad hated the Yankees, didn't he?"

"A lot of folks still do. I bet you can count on one hand the number of Yankee baseball fans here in the county."

"Granddad said Uncle Ray ran and hid in the big cave at Bowden but with no food, he finally had to come out. He was shot by a Yankee officer when he refused to be taken prisoner and tried to escape again."

"That's right. Now, it's late, go to sleep. You can write all this for your essay tomorrow."

"Okay. I'll try. But you know, Granddad told me so many times about two Confederate soldiers being wounded in a skirmish at Bowden. They were carried to his house. His mom was a healer and a mid-wife so folks figured she could help. The soldiers were laid out on the porch and their blood dripped through the cracks in the flooring and stained the dirt below. The bloody stains reminded Granddad of the railroad tracks, and he played in them. He always ended the story with a laugh, saying, 'My mom switched me good for doing that.'"

"Will the two of you stop fighting the Civil War and go to sleep." Mom laughed and then, real soft, she said, "Good night, sleep tight."

"Yeah, go to sleep, son. I think you can write your essay just fine. Now, go to sleep." Dad let out a big yawn and rolled over onto his side with his back to me. Mom sprawled out on my other side. It was like they were saying, *Okay that's enough.*

Dad was right. I knew I could write my essay just fine. Yes, I could compare the wars. I figured wars happen, some people die and others return home. Life goes on and then another war. To stop the clamoring in my brain, I thought of Kate Smith. Big, smiling Kate Smith with the bellowing voice. She was in all the newsreels, sometimes singing at an Army camp or at a bond rally. I remember at supper one evening, laughing, Dad had said, "She would win every hog calling contest in the state if we could just get her to West Virginia."

Mom shushed him, saying, "Be nice. She's a little heavy, but she's so patriotic. And that beautiful voice. She's a national treasure."

I figured I could finish my essay because with Dad's help I had a lot to write about. The thought helped quiet my mind. The low murmur of the fan's whrrrrr was soothing as I felt my eyelids getting heavier and heavier. With Kate Smith's voice softly singing in my sleepy head, *"from the mountains, to the prairies, to the oceans, white with foam,"* I finally fell asleep.

Pages from a Memoir

There is a photograph, taken in 1931, that has been enlarged and fills the page in the family album of my father proudly holding me in his left hand high above his head. I am a baby, wearing a long, white gown that spills down his arm and wrist and onto his shoulders in a soft cloud of lace. My father is so young, in his twenties, handsome and dressed in an open white shirt and dark trousers. I appear to be quite content on my precarious perch, and there is a hint of a smile on my lips.

I have no idea when I became aware that my father was different from other men. Different in that he had only one arm. It was a given, like the Tooth Fairy leaving a dime under your pillow for a lost tooth or Santa Clause bringing you a book and a toy at Christmas if you were truly a good little boy. The Tooth Fairy and Santa Claus became fond memories as I grew older, but my father still had only one arm. He remains in my memory as he was: a physically challenged, handsome, caring, hero of a man.

My father lost his right arm, his good arm as he would say, in a stupid gun accident that was all his fault. He disobeyed his father and used an old shotgun with a broken trigger guard to kill a fox that had been stealing chickens on the farm at Bowden. He arose early one morning before anyone else, took the forbidden shotgun, and climbed on top of the chicken house in the pre-dawn light. The fox appeared, and it took one shot to drop it in its tracks. His father heard the shot, raced from the house, and demanded he hand him the shotgun. My father obeyed, and he reached over the roof edge to hand his father the gun. The unprotected trigger caught on the eave, and the resulting shot was discharged into the shoulder of my father's right arm. He was taken on a hand-pumped railroad car to the hospital eight miles away in Elkins, and, miraculously, he recovered.

He had to learn to live with only his left hand. That meant everything from tying his shoelace with one hand to driving a bulldozer. He conquered these tasks and many, many more with great success.

However, he refused to go back to school in what was to be his eighth grade. This was the last grade taught in the little two room schoolhouse in Bowden. He asked his teacher, "How can I hold a slate and write at the same time? I don't want the other kids to laugh at me."

Fortunately his kind teacher taught him on her own time. "Homer, you're going to have to learn to write your name with your left hand, and you need some more math. Things like the measure of a cord of wood, the volume of a train load of coal, and the heft of a bag of grain or a bushel of apples." He often spoke of her with great respect.

As I was growing up in the country in West Virginia, my father taught me how to hunt and track, to build a deer blind and call a wild turkey. In contrast to his growing up poor on a small mountain farm, he created a childhood of memories for me which I cherish to this day. My mother told me years later, "Your daddy had far more fun hiding the Easter eggs I dyed than you kids had finding them."

He built my brother and me a little log cabin in the woods above our garden that was big enough for sleep overs, and, when we discovered the Tarzan books, he saw that each of us had our own tree house. A big swing hung from the old maple tree in our yard, and in winter he cleared lanes on the ice pond so we could skate. As we grew a bit older, he created a miniature golf course for us. He diverted enough water from the nearby rivulet to create a tiny lake with sandy banks as a trap. He built it as a challenge to our skills and patience. Our friends from town always ended up at our house to use the little golf course or for a game of tag football.

He was always protective of my brother and me. No sports were allowed for us in high school because he was afraid we might get hurt. We both settled for the band. He taught me to walk tall and not be afraid. "I won't always be here for you. You have to do it alone. Be Brave. Be a soldier."

In the summer, before we were old enough to take on mowing lawns and the like, my brother and I were expected to help in the garden, mow and trim the lawn, gather fire wood, clean the chicken house, and what other chores there might be.

He would remind my mother before leaving for work, "Now don't forget, the boys get to read for half an hour on their lunch break."

After lunch, Mother would walk onto the porch, where my brother claimed the swing and I had the glider, to announce, "All right, you can finish the chapter you're reading and then back to work."

We would hear her approach and quickly slip a finger into the next chapter following, thus gaining a little more reading time. Oh, the subterfuge of little boys.

"Have you done your lessons?" It was a daily question of my father to my brother and me. We were expected, from an early age, to borrow books from the library on every imaginable subject. Our parents put great stock in our report cards and followed the subjects we were studying at a particular time.

For me, good grades were a competition not unlike sports for others. Usually I was at or near the head of my class, and I was the winner in my school in the state wide contest for the coveted Golden Horseshoe. The same test is given throughout the state to all eighth grade students at the end of a year's

West Virginia history course. It was begun in 1931 to encourage interest in the state.

The contest was based on the 1716 excursion of some fifty business men commissioned by Governor Spotswood of Virginia to explore the wilds beyond the Shenandoah Valley into what is now West Virginia. The explorers made a wide circle through the mountains noting the available wood, salt, coal deposits and seeking a waterway to the Pacific. Upon their return, the governor gave each participant a little gold lapel pin in the shape of a horseshoe.

The winners are awarded a trip to Charleston and dubbed by the governor a Knight or Lady of the Golden Horseshoe. It is a highly competitive contest, and the victors become instant local celebrities. As reported by West Virginia native Henry Louis Gates in his acclaimed autobiography, *Colored People,* "Winning the Golden Horseshoe in West Virginia is like being awarded the Pulitzer Prize." Yes, I am very proud of my little lapel pin.

This prize helped me to receive a four year, academic scholarship to West Virginia University. My parents were justly proud of my achievement. But things happen. In the spring of my freshman year I was angry at not being rushed by the fraternity of my choice, and I was tired of scrambling at local jobs to keep me in spending money. I had excellent grades but was not guided by my advisor to hang in, to finish the year. Rather, he encouraged me to "follow my heart." I dropped out of the university, forfeiting my scholarship, and took the bus back to Elkins.

That night my parents were very quiet as I explained why I left school. My father took a long look at me and said, ever so quietly, in slow, measured words, "By this time tomorrow you better have a job or you are not welcome in this house."

I hitchhiked to Washington, D.C. the next morning and took a job at a White Tower frying hamburgers. This lasted about six weeks and I was miserable, homesick, and very discouraged. I hitchhiked back to Elkins and was, much to my surprise, welcomed. My father said, "Now get your ass up on the hill and make up your classes. I'll loan you the tuition."

"Up on the hill" meant Davis and Elkins, the excellent, local, Presbyterian college. I finished one summer session and jumped at a job that became available on a Federal project building a dam to protect the city from floods. As the youngest employee, a common day laborer, I worked as hard as at any period in my life. I put in overtime on every possible occasion and banked my salary.

My father advised me once again. "Reapply for your scholarship. Tell them I was ill and needed you so that is why you left school. Now, I'm recovering and you want to continue at Morgantown."

The excuse found a friendly ear at the university, and I was reinstated in my scholarship. The school cafeteria gave me a job again, and I was picked for the Mountaineer Speaking Team whose job was talking to high school students about the university. I also pledged BetaTheta Pi fraternity and continued my studies. English history was my major but it was my minor, theater, that I hoped to pursue. I graduated with my class in 1951.

Little wonder I am proud of my parents who continued to protect, encourage, and advise me.

Be brave. Be a soldier. His words helped me, really more than I knew at the time, in the fall of 1952 when I volunteered for the Army during the Korean War. I heeded his words. I had to. I was scared of going to war. I was in college and exempt as long as I stayed in school. My father tried his best to dissuade me. I vividly remember his plea as he reasoned with me, "Stay in school. You don't have to go."

"But, I think it's my duty." I tried to explain. "One of my roommates in the fraternity house was killed near Pusan this fall. He was calling in mortar fire from the back of a burned out tank when he was shot."

"That's sad but no reason for you to go."

"Daddy, I was at Stub's wedding in June, the week before he shipped out for Korea."

"Listen to me. Finish the semester, graduate, and enroll in law school."

I felt it was my duty to enlist. Things were different then or at least they seem to be as I look back on that long ago fall. I volunteered because I thought it was the right thing to do at the time. Stupid, dumb West Virginia hillbilly? Well, when anyone asks, I always say that next time around I'll take hindsight to good looks any old day.

The American Legion hosted a breakfast for inductees and their parents but my father, still upset with me, refused to attend. He lost his good arm in that stupid gun accident and now, here I was volunteering to go off to possibly get shot. He had good reason to be upset with me.

It was a nice breakfast, and my mother teared up as I boarded the bus for the induction center in Clarksburg. The bus pulled out of the American Legion parking lot and headed up the street before turning onto the highway. And there, on the corner of 2nd Street and Davis Avenue, was my father. He hadn't abandoned me. As the bus passed, he saluted with his left hand. I saluted back. It was the last time I was to see him standing. By New Year's he was in the hospital dying of cancer.

During my week's leave before boarding the troop train in Pittsburgh for the West Coast, my mother gave me my father's wallet. "You know he was set on your going to law school and didn't encourage your acting. But he listened to every broadcast of the radio plays from the university that you were in." She nodded toward the billfold. "Look inside."

Tucked into his worn, leather wallet, folded neatly into little squares were the announcements and reviews of my radio plays. "He always said the acting training would help you in the courtroom when you presented your arguments to the judge and jury."

"Mother, I don't want to go to law school. I want to be an actor."

"Well, we'll see when you get back, won't we? He was so proud of you. You are the first person in his family to graduate college. He loved telling folks, 'My youngest boy is in school down to Morgantown.'"

She started to cry, the only time I saw her lose control all through his illness and death. I joined her that February morning back in 1953 when things did not look the most promising with Korea facing me and knowing I would not be there to help her.

I served my time, mostly in Korea, and was awarded The Combat Infantry Badge, an honor for everyone who comes under enemy fire. It is a tiny replica of a Revolutionary War rifle mounted on a field of blue enamel and encircled with a silver wreath. I wear mine with pride every Veteran's Day. It is my most valued possession.

Fortunately, the Army Personnel Unit discovered that I was a recent college graduate and could type. I was pulled out of Company C that was on line and trained to fill the position of Company Clerk of Headquarters and Headquarters Company of the Regiment. It was a difficult, demanding job and carried great responsibility. But it was a prime assignment and offered me a position of relative safety and an insider's view of the closing days of that hapless war.

Never count on a sure thing, another bit of advice which I have learned to appreciate over the years. I write of this here because a couple of hours after being told of my good fortune by the Company Commander, the First Sergeant crept down the trench line to me. "You and another soldier are to pick up some equipment a few hundred yards down the ridge. The patrol radioed that they dropped ammunition, a machine gun and communications wire, because they weren't needed." Then he laughed at me. "So, you lucky son-of-a-bitch, you're not all that safe after all."

The two of us shouldered our rifles, climbed over the sandbags, and slid down to the ground. It was close to midnight and there was enough starlight to follow the ridge line. We found the dropped equipment easily enough. The other soldier picked up the box of ammunition and slung the bandolier over his shoulder. I did the same with the coil of communications wire and the light machine gun. Loaded down, we headed back up the ridge toward the trench.

We hadn't gone very far when we knew we were being infiltrated by the North Koreans and the Chinese. Almost every night they would slip up close and lob hand grenades toward our trench. We couldn't see or hear them but we could certainly smell them. The odor of their diet of garlic rice and cabbage was overpowering. We didn't hesitate and took off running up the ridge. The other soldier was ahead of me and dropped the ammo box before he climbed up and over the sandbags. My M-1 rifle, the coil of wire, and the light machine were slung over my shoulders which freed up my hands. I, too, scrambled over the formidable barrier and tumbled down into the trench with a clatter.

The First Sergeant was there and he said, "Well, you made it and you didn't drop anything. You're just so damn goody good. Now get your ass out to the listening post. You're not out of here yet."

A listening post is just that—a fox hole some hundred yards or so in front of our trenches. It was manned by two soldiers at a time. We had a small radio and our assignment was listening. Hopefully we would detect any enemy movement and warn of a possible attack. For me, it was as scary as anything you can imagine. Every bush became an enemy soldier crouched for attack, menacing me. Shadows cast by the moon took on a life of their own. I could hear my breathing, uneven, spastic, as my eyes swept back and forth over the mountain terrain in front of me.

The one comforting thought for the rest of that long night was remembering climbing up and over our sandbagged trench line. It was easily eight feet or more high. It seemed to me, as I recalled the climb, there was a strong force under my butt lifting me to safety. Dawn finally arrived, and I crawled back to our trench line. Later that morning I was driven to my assignment.

Months later, when I returned to the States, my brother told me about his son's experience with his granddad. My mother had given my brother and his wife the house that my father was building for retirement on Isner Creek. It was finished in the next months after my father's death, and they moved into their new home the beginning of May.

The first morning after their move, my little nephew David told them at breakfast, "Granddad came to see me last night."

Questioning by my brother and sister-in-law revealed a more detailed explanation. My nephew said, "Granddad was wearing his red checked hunting jacket, and he stood at the foot of the bed and waved to me."

"This is an unlikely story to be made up by a three year old," my brother explained.

My nephew reported two more nightly visits and then they stopped. This timing coincided with my picking up the dropped equipment the night before being pulled back from the front line.

People tell ghost stories and talk of sightings of someone who has recently died or feel their presence. So, I don't know. Ghosts and table tilting and fortune telling are not a part of my life. Not then, nor now. But I do think my father hung around to look after me, to make sure I was all right. His strong left hand helped boost me up and over that formidable, sandbagged trench to safety.

August 2, 1953

The armistice took place at 10:00 p.m., July 27, 1953. Yet it was strangely still in the company area. No shouting, no planned celebration, just an unusually quiet evening. Captain Adams, our company commander, said, "It's too early to celebrate." After a moment he added, "We still have a few men on line."

Captain Adams was a high school math teacher whose gentleness concealed a steel framework. His nickname was The Professor, and he looked the part with his trim stature, round features, and eye glasses. He never made a move until it was well thought out and then executed to perfection.

In contrast, Sergeant Tracy, our First Sergeant, was a banty rooster, aggressive and spirited. To his credit, he knew the name of every soldier in the company. Somehow, the Gods that be had seen fit to assign me the position of Company Clerk and the opportunity to work with these fine gentlemen.

With the approval of Captain Adams, Sergeant Tracy took several cases of beer from supply to the small mountain stream behind our tent. If there was a stream in the area, that's where Sergeant Tracy always set up the Orderly Room Tent. "My beer cooler," he laughed.

I continued to work at my desk with the aid of a kerosine lamp. There was a lot of work accounting for all the men of Headquarters and Headquarters Company of the 5th Regimental Combat Team. It was my job to keep track and report everyone's whereabouts and well being on a daily basis. It was called the Morning Report, a chore seven days a week.

The next day, Monday, dawned bright and early. "It's gonna be another scorcher," I said as I rolled out of my cot and slipped into my fatigues and boots.

"Another hot, steamy day in beautiful Korea." This from grouchy, sleepy Sergeant Tracy. Then, resigned, he muttered his afterthought which said everything about Korea and the day, "Fuck it."

About noon, Captain Adams called a halt to all work and training. "Like the rest of the Regiment, we're gonna celebrate the end of the war."

I kept thinking, this is an armistice but fighting could begin again at any moment. No one seemed concerned about this possibility, so I joined in the celebration.

"The officers of the regiment are planning a late afternoon, evening dinner, and drinks in the officers' mess, and we're gonna have our own celebration. Let's get that beer from the stream." This last was directed to the Supply Sergeant. "We're gonna drive to our swimming hole, and I mean to drink a few beers. This is the end of my second war, and by damn I'm gonna celebrate. You all come with me," and Sergeant Tracy led the way to the jeep parked outside the Orderly Room.

"You all" meant yours truly, the postman, medic, and of course the guys in supply. Another jeep was borrowed from the motor pool, and we took off with the cooled beer.

Sergeant Tracy used our field telephone to call other companies. As the afternoon wore on, we were joined by about fifteen sergeants, all of them downing beer after beer. I nursed one beer for I knew I still had a good deal of work awaiting me.

Soon a number of the sergeants, led by Sergeant Tracy, began pushing men into the water, clothes, boots, and all. Every newcomer to the spontaneous beer blast got dunked. A tipsy Sergeant Tracy was himself picked up and tossed into the pool.

"You bastards," he laughed as he sloshed out of the water, beer in hand. Dripping wet, he turned to his old buddy from World War II and shoved him into the pool. "Have a bath and celebrate, you tired fuck."

Sergeant Tracy's old friend was the First Sergeant of Love Company. The two of them had parachuted into France before D-Day. They had survived and were decorated by Eisenhower for their bravery. At this time both men were probably mid-forties and regular army. Sergeant Tracy had received a battlefield promotion to Major but after the war ended, he opted to return to his old rank as a non-commissioned officer. I was fortunate to be assigned to his company.

One evening, after too many beers during one of our many bull sessions in the orderly room tent, I said, "You remind me of my dad. Except my dad didn't drink."

"Then how the hell do I remind you of him?"

"My dad lost his arm in a gun accident when he was about twelve or so. He learned to do about everything a man has to do. He would show his workmen that he could accomplish a given task. If he could do it, then why couldn't they? His workmen respected him for that and worked all the harder. And, Sergeant Tracy, you're like that."

"Whatta you want, a promotion?" He laughed. "Well, I can't promote you, but I can say you're a damn good company clerk." Then he had gotten up from his cot and moved to clank his beer can against mine.

No more was ever said, but I liked him and we worked well together. I told myself over and over, *I am one lucky guy. I have a great job, am reasonably safe, and what a terrific place to observe the war.* You see, my father had died that January and just five weeks later I shipped out for Korea. I guess, in a way, Sergeant Tracy had become a surrogate father to me.

Two days later we were told we would be moving further back, below the 38th parallel, the decided division line between North and South Korea. It was raining and continued right through the morning of our move on August 1st. The dirt roads were muddy and a mess and made for slow going. I always traveled with Captain Adams, Sergeant Tracy, and our driver. Of course my metal, collapsible desk was tied onto the rear of the jeep. It held the records of the company and was awarded priority status.

Usually, Captain Adams chose to lead the convoy on any move. Today, because of the condition of the roads, he had us about one third of the way into the column. "In this weather and with these roads, I want to be where I can be on call quickly if needed."

Suddenly, at mid morning, the column ground to a halt. We were on a high, narrow, muddy road climbing slowly around a good sized mountain. As our driver pulled to a stop, several soldiers came running back from the vehicles stopped in front of us.

"There's been an accident, Sir."

"Sir, a big truck is over the hill. We've got injured. Doc Manos is there."

Doc Manos was our company medic, a sergeant and a fine soldier. Captain Adams leaped out of the jeep and was quickly joined by Sergeant Tracy. I grabbed my carry bag containing a notebook and pencils and followed. Just around the bend and perhaps seven vehicles ahead of our jeep, we saw the heavy, two-ton truck of the Communications Platoon wrecked down the steep embankment. Soldiers were attempting to right the big vehicle which had crushed a number of the men riding in the canvas covered truck bed.

Doc had already radioed Seoul for help and was tending to a badly cut soldier. Bodies were strewn like randomly broken dolls about the muddy hillside where they had been thrown from the truck. Within minutes a helicopter from Division headquarters landed nearby. A doctor and two male nurses quickly moved from the copter to aid the injured.

"I'm gonna check the dog tags of everyone who is hurt." Captain Adams motioned to me, "You make sure I get 'em right."

"Yes, sir," I replied and started writing out the names of the soldiers as we moved along the steep hillside. Suddenly, I stopped, my hand began to shake and I could not write.

Captain Adams looked at me and asked, "What is it?"

Barely able to speak, I said, "It's Skipper. He's from West Virginia, my good friend. We talk every day."

"I'm sorry. But we have to go on."

"Yes, sir. Oh, God, his wife just had a baby." Now, I was crying, unable to control myself.

Captain Adams put his arm across my shoulders and pulled me close to him. "Here, give me your tablet."

"No, Sir. I'm okay. I'm okay." I took in the scene down the hillside where the medics were being aided by soldiers who had piled out of our convoy trucks. I forced myself to go on. "It's all right, Sir. Let's continue."

"You're sure?"

"Yes, Sir." Slowly, he moved onto the next body, and I followed. Somehow, I finished writing down all the names. I still don't know how I managed that. I sat on the ground, waiting while Captain Adams spoke with the doctor. It seemed like a long while as I kept reading the list of names over and over. Finally, Sergeant Tracy led me back to our jeep.

Eight men had injuries serious enough to need hospital care. Arrangements were made to transport those men to a hospital in Seoul, about thirty-five miles to the south. The four bodies of the dead were taken to Division headquarters.

A greatly saddened convoy then continued our slow journey toward our assigned assembly site.

Our new campground was north of Seoul about twenty-five miles. Captain Adams explained, "We're part of a buffer line protecting the capital from a possible renewal of the war and assault from North Korea."

Sergeant Tracy chimed in, "I said to anybody who'd listen that this was a truce. This damn thing might not be over yet."

These were exactly my thoughts of the last several days, but I said nothing. All I could think of was Skipper's body sprawled on the hillside.

"All right, Sergeant, but let's be optimistic and hope for the best." Captain Adams' voice had a slight edge. "I wanna get home. My oldest boy starts high school this fall."

"Yes, Sir," Sergeant Tracy immediately backed away from more negative comments and set about organizing our company area.

"Phillips, get out your report as soon as you can. We'll set up a canvas cover for your office until we can get our tent for the orderly room".

"Yes, sir. I have all the names, but I want to go over them with the platoon sergeant. Just to make sure we get it right."

"Good thought. We've got eight men injured and four dead. What a sad day."

"Yes, sir. I was told the road just gave way under that heavy truck. It wasn't the driver's fault."

"I can't make a call on that until I talk with the driver and the survivors. Of course Division will decide. I do know our boys had to shore up the road before the heavier equipment was brought through. Damn, what a miserable day. And I'm sorry about your friend."

All I could say was, "Yes, Sir. I'll get busy. There's a lot to do. I'll have to write his wife, of course."

"The colonel wants a report as soon as possible. That goes for Division and probably the 1st Army as well. What a mess.

What a goddamned mess. Six days thinking we're safe, and I lose four men." Captain Adams' face was drawn tight, his voice contrite.

Sergeant Tracy soon appeared with a large canvas, some poles, and men from AT&M to set up a cover for my desk. AT&M were the initials for the Anti-Tank and Mine Platoon. However, the platoon was made up mostly of carpenters and workmen who could build and repair just about anything needed by our Regiment.

I watched the men erect the cover as I set up my little office. The trunk unfolded into a desk set on four, metal-footed legs. It had been my home since mid May when Unit Personnel discovered I was a college graduate and could type.

"You lucky son-of-a-bitch," was the only remark I had received from my First Sergeant in Company C. That was where I had been assigned after landing at Inchon that early April.

I set about the sad but necessary detailed report of the accident and the roster of the dead and injured soldiers who were riding in the truck that morning. It was my job, and it was a rough one. Every so often, a chill shook my body, and I had to wait a moment before continuing. Skipper had gone through basic training with me and when we discovered we both were from West Virginia, we became fast friends. He wasn't the first friend I had lost. Bud Kramer had been wounded during an attack two days after I had been pulled back to become Company Clerk. He was now recovering in a hospital in Tokyo. Bud had written that he was going home soon. Skipper would be going home, too, but in a box.

I continued with my report as I remembered so well families being notified by telegram of the loss of a son or father in World War II. There were several gold star banners hanging in windows along my paper route. The mother of one of the soldiers never answered her front door again. On collection day I would find the money under the porch rug.

Now the happy relief of the truce for four families would be shattered with telegrams from the War Department. With a deep sigh, I finished and tucked the completed brief under my poncho and walked it to S-2, the intelligence offices of the Regiment.

Due to helping set up our big tent, none of us got much sleep. It had stopped raining and before breakfast I trudged to the headquarters tent to pick up our daily reports. I quickly scanned the accident report from Division. My stomach did a massive jump, and I staggered to a dead stop as I read. We had two men named MacCumber in the Communications Platoon, and the wrong man was reported dead on the Division roster.

Quickly I checked my report, and it correctly listed Private John H. MacCumber. The Division papers clearly listed David M. MacCumber as deceased. Frantically, I set out in a run to find Captain Adams, the papers clutched tightly in my hand.

I trailed after Captain Adams as we reported to S-2. We had to wait a few minutes for the Colonel. When he arrived, we saluted and Captain Adams quickly explained the situation of the wrong man being reported as dead.

The Colonel butted in as he pushed back his chair and jumped to his feet, "Where the hell was your head, Corporal? How in God's name could you make a mistake like this?"

"Sir-" Captain Adams tried to explain but was overridden by the Colonel.

"I'll have you courtmartialed for this," the Colonel yelled. "What a stupid ass mistake. This is a blot on my record. A huge--"

"Sir, the mistake was made at Division or Army." Captain Adams' voice finally silenced the Colonel. "Perhaps I wasn't clear in my explanation. Corporal Phillips' report is accurate. I'm proud of him, and he caught the mistake before breakfast this morning."

"Oh?" The Colonel looked confused. "You mean we're, that is, our report is accurate?"

"Yes, Sir."

"We're not to blame? Well, that's good news. Good news, indeed, Captain." The Colonel turned to Major Harmon, head of S-2, "Get me 3rd Division headquarters."

"Yes, Sir." Major Harmon quickly moved to the telephone.

"Serious business. This is damn serious for us." The Colonel seated himself and began to shift through a pile of papers on his desk.

"Sir, may I dismiss Corporal Phillips? He has work to do."

"Oh, yes, of course. But you, Adams, stay here in case I need you to talk to Division."

"Thank you, Sir." I saluted and fled from the big tent, happy to be out of the presence of our not-so-dearly loved Regimental Commander. "What a miserable fuck," was all I could think of as I headed back to the Orderly Room.

Colonel Johnson had recently replaced our commanding officer who had rotated back to the States. Our former commander visited his men on the front line every day. He frequently walked the entire trench line assigned to the 5th RCT. I had met him briefly back in April when I was still assigned to Company C on line.

But the new Colonel was, simply put, a pain in the ass. He rarely visited the men under his command and was short-tempered to say the least. Lee, the Korean houseboy assigned to the Orderly Room, reported to Sergeant Tracy that the Colonel had struck Jimbo, his houseboy, because the kid had scorched one of his shirts. Jimbo told his Korean buddies that in retaliation, he pissed in every newly opened bottle of the Colonel's drink of choice, Scotch.

Captain Adams, laughing all the while, told Sergeant Tracy and me the story of the recent welcoming party thrown by the Colonel for Regimental Officers.

"I've never heard of an entire command staff drinking only canned beer. I offered my good Scotch and bourbon and all of them refused. I've never seen this before in any of my assignments." This was the gist of the Colonel's statement to Captain Adams.

Of course the Korean houseboys had told everyone in the Company and word spread quickly through the Regiment about Jimbo pissing in his bosses' liquor. Naturally the officers switched to canned beer when in attendance to the Colonel. It was a story that relieved the boredom and took the edge off homesickness for all of the Regiment.

In a very short time, Captain Adams appeared to brief Sergeant Tracy and me. "Phillips, Colonel Johnson didn't even thank you for doing a good job. What an ass. He doesn't deserve the command of this regiment. I apologize for him and say thank you once again for your work."

I was grateful to this fine man and mumbled a quiet, "Thank you, Sir."

Captain Adams noted my barely audible response and asked, "Are you all right, Corporal?"

"Yes, sir, I'm okay. It's such a shock. I mean the war is over and..." I stopped, unable to go on.

"It's tough, Phillips. Things happen. But we soldier on."

"Yes, Sir. Thank you for your consideration."

Captain Adams reached to touch my shoulder before he continued. "Chaplain Irons wants a memorial service for those we lost. I suggested this evening. Any thoughts on this, Sergeant Tracy?"

"I say, good timing. Three of the injured will be coming back to us tomorrow. We'll also have a full report from Seoul on the recovery schedule of the other men. So, yes, good timing."

"Glad you agree. We need some kind of closure on this." Captain Adams removed his glasses and placed them carefully on his desk. As he pressed his fingers against his eye lids, he continued. "Hell, I need closure. This happened on my watch."

"Sir, you didn't have any control over that truck or that road. You're doing all you can."

"Sergeant, I know that. But still..." Captain Adams' voice failed him. After a moment, once more in command, he said, "Chaplain Irons suggested that we encourage buddies of those dead and injured to speak; that is, if they choose to. I plan to say something. God knows what but I have to try to help."

"Sir, I can only say thanks to you and Chaplain Irons. The Communications Platoon is hurting real bad with the loss. We all are. And Phillips lost his buddy. We shared daily duties, and now we are facing the absence of twelve men every single day. Not easy to do. Not at all."

"Thanks for your support, Sergeant." Captain Adams took a moment, looked at his notes, and then went on to explain what was to happen. "Here's the plan. A Colonel from Division Headquarters in Seoul will fly up this evening along with a doctor. A telephone call will be cleared to enable Private MacCumber to speak with his family. In turn, an Army doctor will be sent to MacCumber's family home to be in attendance when the call goes through. His family lives in a small town in Texas near Dallas."

"Will the call be placed from here or S-2?" Sergeant Tracy, as always a practical planner, interrupted. "And a doctor? Why?"

"Army policy for a doctor to be in attendance for any possible need. We'll accompany Private MacCumber this evening. This is one helluva mistake. I can't begin to imagine how the boy's family will receive the news. Good news, obviously. But to find out that your son who you thought had been killed is alive and coming home? Boy, what a fucked up situation."

"MacCumber is being sent home?" Again, Sergeant Tracy, nailing down specifics.

"Yes, he deserves that. He'll also be given a thirty day furlough which will be in addition to normal leave time. Of course, he will have to serve out his enlistment." Then, to me, "Corporal, he is Regular Army? Right?"

"Yes, Sir. He enlisted last fall. This is his first assignment."

"Well, at least he'll serve his time in the States. I wouldn't be at all surprised to see him assigned to a camp in Texas. I mean, we've, that is the Army, has thrown one helluva curve to him and his family."

"We'll brief MacCumber on all of this?"

"Absolutely. Ask him to meet me here this morning. This will give him time to think about the coming phone call to his family."

"Yes, Sir." With a quick salute, Sergeant Tracy strode out to alert Private MacCumber.

"Anything else for me this morning, Corporal?"

"No, Sir. We're good for now."

"I want you to attend this evening because you're the obvious person to write up a report for me. Of course S-2 will file their report, but I want one from our Company. For now, at least, this is Private MacCumber's home."

"Yes, Sir."

Captain Adams sat at his desk and busied himself with the various reports I had gotten earlier from Major Harmon. It was now eight-thirty or so, and I was hungry. "I'm going to get a sandwich and coffee. I haven't eaten this morning. Would you like some coffee, Sir?"

"Good of you to ask, but, no, thanks."

I saluted as I left the Orderly Room and headed for the Mess Tent. All I could think of was writing a letter to Eleanor, Skipper's wife. How could I do that? "What a day," I said aloud as I walked across the company area. "And it's just begun."

Right after lunch, Captain Adams briefed Sergeant Tracy and me on the day's events thus far. "Private MacCumber took the news like the fine young man he appears to be. He graduated high school last year with a B average, and he made the All State track team. And he's a golfer. We talked about that. Truly, I don't think he understands the shock this is to his family, but we'll see. He's of course delighted to being sent Stateside so soon and not facing nine months over here."

Sergeant Tracy spoke up, "I like the boy, and his Platoon Sergeant gave me an excellent report on him."

"Well, all that sounds good. Major Harmon tells me the headquarters tent is being readied for the phone call and the welcoming of the officers from Division. A Colonel Adams and a Major Williams, a doctor. Maybe we can lighten things a bit with our names both being Adams." With a laugh, he continued. "Except I'm a lowly Captain and can't wait to be discharged and work on my golf game."

I welcomed the Captain's smile for they had been sparse in recent days. I liked and respected him a great deal and, as with Sergeant Tracy, we worked well together.

"So, are we set for this evening?" He continued, "I'll meet you both here with Private MacCumber, and we'll walk together to S-2. I think it's important for Intelligence to know we support MacCumber in every possible way. The four of us appearing together will let the Colonel from Division know that as well."

"And our fucking, Scotch loving commander." Sergeant Tracy guffawed, "Oh, God, if he knew about Jimbo."

Captain Adams quickly added, another broad smile on his face, "Is there some way I can award a medal to Jimbo, do you think?"

More laughter from the three of us–a desperately needed moment of lightness which had been so lacking since the wreck of the truck.

Promptly at seventeen and a half hours, the four of us set out. All of us were in dress uniforms, that is, no fatigues but khaki shirts and trousers for all, including Captain Adams. Lee had ironed all of our uniforms earlier in the afternoon.

Both Captain Adams and Sergeant Tracy wore their respective ribbons with the Sergeant's covering the full left side of his shirt. I could plainly see a Purple Heart and a Silver Star among the many ribbons. I wore only my Combat Infantry Badge. It is awarded to any soldier who comes under enemy fire.

The badge is a tiny replica of a Revolutionary War rifle mounted on a small square of blue enamel and surrounded by a silver wreath. I was qualified to wear it because of the incoming mortar and artillery fire when on line in Company C. It was now my proudest possession.

As planned, the four of us entered the big tent together. Captain Adams stopped in front of Colonel Johnson, saluted, and said, "Sir, Captain Adams reporting as ordered." The three of us saluted as well, each stating our name as we did.

I was surprised to see the spruced up interior of the big tent. The five desks of the Colonel, Major, and three clerks had been set around the perimeter of the tent. The center tent pole had a field telephone taped securely in place about four feet from the ground with folding chairs spaced about it. I thought, I could use one of those. The seat I had was a shipping crate rescued from the Mess Tent. I smiled as I remembered the stamped POTATOES sign on its sides. The crate reminded me pretty much on a daily basis of my uncle Okey. He was on KP at Pearl Harbor and years later he said to me, "You ever see *From Here to Eternity?*"

"Sure," I said.

"Well, that shot of the Jap plane machine gunning the boardwalk is just the way it was. I had dived for cover under the Mess Hall and watched the bullets cutting that walkway right down the middle. Thank God the plane pulled up before reaching us."

The December 7th attack on Pearl Harbor was broadcast over the radio all that Sunday. My dad had paced our living room, back and forth, back and forth. I was twelve at the time, and it remains a vivid memory.

The eight chairs were dwarfed by the height of the large tent. Light was provided by kerosene lamps suspended by wire hooks from cloth loops sewn along the seams of the tent. It was a dramatic arrangement, and I thought how like a stage set it appeared or a scene for a Hollywood movie. Except this was for real. No role playing for actors.

As I finished my appraisal of the space the gruff voice of Sergeant Tracy broke the quiet: "At-ten-shun." We stood and saluted as the officers filed into the tent. I noticed that the doctor from Division was a Major. I thought, nothing like a mistake to bring out the heavy artillery: two Colonels, two Majors, and a Captain. I glanced at Private MacCumber. He appeared as impressed as I was, his mouth agape as he stared at the officers.

Colonel Johnson introduced Colonel Adams and Major Williams, a doctor, from Division Headquarters. Everyone shook hands, and Colonel Adams nodded toward the chairs, "Have a seat gentlemen." As we took seats, he reached his hand out to Private MacCumber. "And you, young man. Private MacCumber is it?"

"Yes, Sir." MacCumber turned to face the Colonel.

"We'll be placing a call to your family, as I'm sure you know. A doctor is with your family. You'll be asked to state your full name, rank, and serial number. Once you've done that, then your mother or father will be handed the telephone. Is that clear?"

"Yes, Sir."

"They tell me you were a track star in high school."

"Yes, Sir."

"I did that, too. I was a long distance runner at Virginia Tech. Cross country through those beautiful hills. I loved it. What was your event?"

"Well, Sir, I was more of a sprinter. The 440 was my best. But we all ran cross country." He smiled at the Colonel. There was a brief pause, then MacCumber blurted, "Sir," as the smile slid from his face.

Colonel Adams appeared not to notice the delayed courtesy of "Sir," and said, "Good man. Sprinters always amazed me. Great sport, running. I still do a couple of miles every morning. Not as fast as I used to be. But it gets the kinks out, gets me ready for the day."

"Yes, Sir."

"I should say, when I can, because-"

Major Harmon interrupted, "Sir. I have Texas on the phone for you."

"Good man."

I watched as Colonel Adams reached to take the field telephone from Major Harmon. He's a good officer, I thought.

"Sir, this is Colonel Adams here of Third Division. Are you gentlemen all set?" There was a brief pause, and he turned to MacCumber. "Private, step up here. Now remember, you'll be asked first to identify yourself and then you'll speak with your folks. Ready?"

"Yes, Sir. I understand."

I thought MacCumber looked a little frightened when the Colonel placed the telephone firmly in his hand.

"Go ahead, Private. And speak up." The Colonel stepped back and clasped his hands behind his back, his feet spread wide in parade rest.

"Hello," and MacCumber paused. With a furtive glance at the Colonel, he stammered, "Private David M. MacCumber, US52194519." Again a brief pause as he listened. Then, quickly, he said, "Manning. Manning is my middle name, Sir."

It was deadly quiet in the big tent. I looked around, and everyone was focused on Private MacCumber. Both Captain

Adams and Sergeant Tracy were seated on the front of their respective chairs. Each of them leaned forward, as though they were ready to leap to help MacCumber. I was holding my breath. Slowly I exhaled and tried to relax, pulling my shoulders down from where they were hunched up about my ears. I tried to lean back in my chair but found myself leaning in toward Private MacCumber as well.

Anticipating the coming telephone call, I remembered my father's plea last fall as he reasoned with me to, "Stay in school. You don't have to go."

"But, I think it's my duty. Besides," I tried to explain, "one of my roommates in the fraternity house, Stub, was killed near Pusan."

"That's sad, but no reason for you to get shot."

"I was at Stub's wedding to Mary Ann. It was in June, the week before he shipped out for Korea."

"Listen to me, please. You finish the semester and enroll in law school."

I had volunteered for the draft anyway. It was against his will, and he was truly upset. But then he got sick, and all was forgiven. Now, here I was, waiting to hear another guy talk with his dad.

"Mother?" It was a question that took everyone by surprise. All of us glanced at one another as the word, common to each of us, shattered the quiet.

"Mother, it's me, David." He continued in a rush, "I'm coming home. They think next week." In a louder voice, he went on, "No, listen, Mama, it's me, David, and I'm coming home." He stopped and looked at Sergeant Tracy.

"Go on, Son. Talk." Sergeant Tracy's voice was impatient, hoarse as he pointed to MacCumber, flipping his fingers encouraging him to speak.

"What? Dad?" MacCumber had quickly placed the telephone to his ear again. "Dad, is Mama okay? What? Grammy?

You want Grammy's name? It's Irene. Grammy Irene. Oh, Daddy, it's me, David." MacCumber's voice was strong, argumentative as he continued. "What? My dog? Brandy. His name is Brandy, and he's a Border Collie. I named him because the first day I had him he chewed the label off your brandy bottle. Remember?" A pause, again. MacCumber continued, "Oh, Daddy, it's me, David. David." MacCumber's earlier confidence crumbled, and he began to cry, big gulping sobs as he leaned against the tent pole, the telephone pressed tight against his cheek.

Major Williams quickly stepped forward. He slipped his arm across MacCumber's shoulders and with his other hand he took the telephone and handed it to Colonel Adams. He murmured, "It's all right, son. It's all right."

"Mr. MacCumber, this is Colonel Adams, Third Division, Korea." The Colonel paused briefly, then continued, "Your son, David, is just fine. He's a tribute to your good name, sir." Another moment and he said, "Next week. You will be alerted just as soon as the orders are cut. Are you all right, Sir? And Mrs. MacCumber?" Again, a pause. "That's good. My regards to you and all your family. Would you put the doctor on for me?" He looked to see that MacCumber was all right before he continued. "Are you okay there? Can we terminate this now?" Colonel Adams exhaled a big breath, "Whew." Then, once again he spoke into the telephone. "Good. Things are under control here, too. Thank you for your help." He placed the telephone into the webbed case and turned to face all of us seated about the tent pole. Quickly he crossed to place his hand on MacCumber's shoulder.

MacCumber looked up, stammered, "Sir, I'm sorry, but Daddy needed proof that it was really me." The tears were streaming down his face.

"You did fine, young man. I'm proud of you. Your folks are so happy and you'll be seeing them soon." He turned to Major Harmon. "I think we're all okay with this. Right?"

Major Harmon looked at Colonel Johnson who nodded. "Yes, Sir. We're good. I know you have to get back to Seoul. We're most grateful for you taking the time to fly up here. Deeply grateful, Sir."

Captain Adams stood and motioned to us. He tilted his head to us as though to say, "Let's go." He stepped to MacCumber seated with Major Harper beside him.

"Let's go home, David." Captain Adams' voice was as gentle as I had ever heard it. "Your buddies are waiting for you. They'll want a full report." He took MacCumber's hand and turned to face Colonel Johnson. "With your permission, Sir."

"Of course, Captain." With this dismissal, he nodded to the Colonel and the Major from Division, then guided them out of the tent.

"At-ten-shun," rang out from Sergeant Tracy. As the officers left he laughed, and murmured to me, "I guess he'll offer them a drink."

Later, in the Communications tent, MacCumber excitedly told his buddies of the meeting with the Colonel and related, almost verbatim, the conversation with his folks.

I helped Sergeant Tracy carry two cases of beer to the tent. He and Captain Adams sat with the men sharing a beer and talking about the accident. They were soon joined by Chaplain Irons who led a brief, touching memorial for the four men killed in the accident. I thought he did a great job in that he knew the home town of every one of the deceased. And no notes. Good man.

"Gentlemen, I bring good news. All of our men are doing well and will enjoy full recovery. Three of them will come back here tomorrow. And yes, I will have a beer with you. So relax, all of you." This was met by laughter that the Chaplin joined.

I stayed for one beer, watching and listening to the men as they began to shake off the loss of their four friends. I decided not to say anything but instead left it to Skipper's platoon buddies to pay him tribute.

As I slipped away to compose my record of the evening's phone call I felt as though a rope was being tightened about my head and my shoulders ached with tension. "Dear Eleanor" kept repeating and repeating in my head.

In the Orderly Room, Doc was already asleep and the Supply Sergeant and our post office guy, Tony, were deeply engaged in a game of chess. I didn't want to type because of Doc sleeping, so I tried to make a beginning in my notebook. It was a useless effort. I looked at the words, scribbled on my pad. Stupidly, I had written, "Once upon a time."

Suddenly, my mind was flooded with the children's rhyme: *Ring-a-round the rosie, A pocket full of posies, Ashes! Ashes! We all fall down.* As kids, we recited this as we played, circling, holding hands. Then, at the end of the rhyme, with *all fall down*, we would scatter and fall into grotesque poses of death. I could picture our front yard and the kids scattered about in contorted positions. This recalled anew our truck wrecked two days earlier with broken bodies strewn down the hillside. The memory of a children's game now turned into a macabre reality with the letter to be composed to Eleanor, a haunting duty weighing me down.

All this opened the slow healing wound of the loss of my father. I knew I was going to cry, so I fled the orderly room and ran to the stream behind our tent. I had made a little seat on a rock there and it was my place of refuge. I was crying now, out of control, my face wet with tears.

I looked at the stream flowing silently into the darkness and murmured, "Six months until I rotate home."

The darkness was a comfort, a protective cover as I recalled my emergency leave during basic training. They put me on an Army transport flying to Pittsburgh that same day. My uncle Leo met me and drove us to Elkins. That night I sat with my father, holding his hand. My mother, exhausted with the two week vigil, slept in another room.

Toward morning, Daddy mumbled, barely audible to me, his voice rasping from the morphine, "Mama, Mama? Can I have the blue bicycle in the window? At Montgomery Ward? Can I?" In his delirium, he thought I was his mother.

I said, "Yes, Homer. You can have the bicycle."

A tiny smile graced his lips for a moment. The bicycle he had bought for my older brother for his tenth birthday had been blue.

My father died that morning at 8:17.

Now, sitting along the stream in the darkness in Korea, haunted by the trauma of the last few days, I felt so close to him. "Can you hear me, Daddy?" My voice was a plea, a little shaky like Private MacCumber's had been. "My dog's name is Boots. You named her that because she had four white paws. Her name is Boots, Daddy."

River with the Banks Falling In

Rose Marie hugged her parka tightly about her and, in spite of the cold, paused halfway up the snow-banked walk leading to the hospital. Salt crystals crackled beneath her boots as she turned slowly to gaze at the encircling mountains. Covered with a blanket of snow, the mountains seemed so near that Rose Marie felt she could reach to touch them.

The mountains were part of her life, so close, breathtaking in their towering beauty. Still, with all their giant majesty, they hid deceitful chasms filled with thick laurel and gave no warning as powerful streams poured off their steep slopes when rainstorms formed about their summits. She thought of the farm where Kelly Mountain rose like a sudden wall, pushing upward on the far bank of Isner Creek. She missed it all so much. The mountain, the farm, and the creek.

After Donald had gotten lost for the second time in the car, they put the farm up for sale and moved into town. Donald got lost in town, too. At least in town he was walking, not driving, and most folks knew him. Neighbors could direct him back to the house or call Rose Marie if there was a problem. The disease would progress, she knew that, but at what rate was anybody's guess. The minister reminded Rose Marie that each day was a gift to be lived in the best possible way, to treasure and not to wait until tomorrow to celebrate their life together. She tried to remember that.

Thankfully, they found an old house just a few blocks from the hospital. The house was small with no basement or central heating, so the rent was surprisingly low and, to their joy, the backyard sloped to the river. They immediately began to feed the wild ducks paddling in circles in the pool shaded by a giant hemlock. During the seventies the house had been worked on by a young hippie couple who paneled the downstairs rooms with hickory and installed a huge wood stove on a native limestone hearth. The stove inspired Donald to chop up all the wood in sight.

Rose Marie moved her boot across the icy walk, testing its slickness, thinking, *the roads will be bad*. Her son would be driving in over the weekend with his family, and Donald's daughter had promised to visit from up the Valley. As always, she told herself not to waste time worrying. *What will be, will be.* She formed the words softly as her father had taught her from the time she was a little girl. Her father had moved the two of them back to West Virginia after her mother died in the early thirties during the Great Depression. That bleak period when the world huddled in desperation, wondering if the good times would ever return. Seventy years had gone by so quickly, and now she and Donald were in their eighties.

It was their mutual respect and love for the wilds that brought Donald and her together some forty years earlier on a rafting trip down the Cheat River. On the first night of the outing while seated around a campfire and playing word games, Donald described a life-long ambition in his growl of a voice.

"Just once in my life, I'd like to be able to climb inside a tree. To peel back the bark and step right inside and wrap myself in it."

They all laughed at his imaginative thought. Rose Marie knew at that moment that he was special. Reliving the moment, she stood a little taller, careful not to slip on the ice. The crisp, early morning air roughed her cheeks and sent a shiver across her shoulders. A small smile curved her lips and softened her face as she thought of the brown paper bag clutched in her hand.

She tucked a wind-blown strand of silver hair under her parka hood, adjusted the strap of her shoulder bag, and carefully continued up the snowy walk to the hospital.

Like many women of the town, she had been a volunteer here for years. Now, she would be the one viewed from behind half-opened doors by the staff. Not as a volunteer but as a worried visitor.

It's my turn now, she thought. *I'm on the other side of the fence*.

Rose Marie quietly entered Donald's room on the second floor. He was sleeping on his back, his long, curly, white hair softly framing his face in sharp contrast to his bushy, black eyebrows.

"He looks good," Rose Marie whispered to the nurse's aide.

"He slept real well, Mrs. Calain. Woke up some but went to sleep again with no fret. Had a good night. Let us know if you need anything," she whispered and slipped quietly from the room.

Rose Marie hung up her parka and pulled the chair closer to the bed and removed the package from the brown paper bag.

Donald opened his eyes and looked up at her as she did so. He pulled himself up on the pillows as high as the restraints around his wrists would allow, his eyes, big and round, quizzical. "Did they beat up on you, too?" Donald asked.

His expression reminded her of their meeting. The night around the camp fire when he talked about climbing inside a tree. And now, the intense questioning once again.

"What are you raving about?" Rose Marie said gently, checking if the knotted cloth was cutting into his hands.

"Beat up on me they did. Kicked me something awful in my side."

"Donald," she was firm but determined not to preach, "you had a kidney stone taken out. Nobody beat up on you. Put that right out of your head."

"You watch out," his voice was low and conspiratorial, "they'll get you, too."

"They operated on you, and your side hurts 'cause that's where they took out the stone." She placed the gift-wrapped box on the bed and reached for her purse.

"You mean they didn't beat up on me?" He rolled his head in the nest of pillows and looked directly at her.

His deep blue eyes took her breath for a moment. No matter how he aged, she saw the young man in his eyes. She hated to have him restrained, but she would have hated it more if he pulled out the catheter. Twice since the operation he had yanked the IV from his arm. He could seriously injure himself if he did the same with the catheter.

"Honey, you're in the Davis Memorial Hospital, and you're sore from the operation." She removed the paper from her purse and unfolded the sign she had printed.

YOU ARE IN THE HOSPITAL.
YOU HAD THE BIGGEST KIDNEY STONE
EVER REMOVED.

She had underlined the EVER in red and drawn little hearts in each corner. At the bottom of the sign were the words,

HAPPY VALENTINE'S DAY.

"I'm going to pin this to the foot of the bed for you." She began to attach the sign to the metal footboard with clothespins that she also took from her purse. "Leave it to you to have the biggest stone they ever seen."

"Where is it?" His eyes were now clear, and she knew that he understood. "I wanna see it."

"Well, you can't see it, honey. They sent it down to Morgantown for tests. To the lab."

"Tests? They didn't ask me if they could test it. And for what? Anyway, hell, it's outta me now."

"Don't swear. Just 'cause you're sick don't give you leave."

Rose Marie pulled her sweater tight across her shoulders. The winter sun was a flat, cool grayness slanting through the window bringing no warmth to the room. She felt she hadn't been truly warm since the day before Thanksgiving when the doctor had diagnosed Donald as having Alzheimer's.

"Ah, old-timers," Donald had quipped.

Only three short months and already he forgot more frequently. Most times, he could sort through the darkening shadows of memory and pick up the pieces of a thought, then slowly wrestle his way back to the present.

"Every case is different," Doc McNeil had told her. "He could stabilize for months or progress rapidly. We just don't know."

"What's that?" Donald eyed the package.

"It's from Henry. From New York. And I bet you can guess what it is."

"No, I can't." He hesitated and then, "Henry?"

"Henry. Henry Isner. He told you he'd send you something when he was here Christmastime."

"He did?"

"Oh, honey, yes. Don't you remember? You know Henry. Your cousin."

Donald stared up at her blankly.

"Your hats? One you wanted and didn't have?"

"Well, open it. You notice I can't since they got me hog-tied here in this dumb bed."

"That's to keep you from pulling out the catheter. I'm sorry, honey, but we got to do it."

"Let's see what it is?" Donald hunched up further on the pillows, keeping his eyes on the package.

Rose Marie undid the string and the tape and opened the gift-wrapped box. Slowly she pulled the tissue paper away. "Well, now look at that. New York Yankees."

"Where do you see that?" Donald squinted at the hat.

"The N and the Y together on top of each other."

"Looks like Japanese to me."

"Oh, honey, look. The Y is over the N so you read it New York and then read the Y again for the Yankees."

"Well, they lost anyhow." Donald grunted in disgust, "Huh. That other team up there won."

"Honey, I know, you told me that. You don't like them, but you needed it for your collection. Let me put it on you." She brushed his hair back with her fingers and cocked the cap over his right eye. "Well, it looks real good on you."

"Yeah? Doggone. Henry sent it, eh?"

"And now we can hang it."

"Hang it? Where? On the coat rack? It's full now. And you won't let me put up a wire." The last was a simple statement. Even in his illness he didn't complain to her.

"Honey, the wire is up. Stretched right around the dining room and into the hallway just the way you wanted."

"It's up?"

"You bet it is."

Donald cocked his head at an angle, peering at her as though from a great depth. "I must be gettin' worse, eh? I don't remember."

There were times Rose Marie felt he knew her thoughts even before they were expressed. She gave a little laugh to cover his hitting so close to the truth. "I just did it. While you've been here. It's to celebrate your coming home. Doc McNeil says Saturday. And we'll hang each hat as it strikes your fancy."

"All of 'em?"

"Every single one. I figure that way we can get a count on how many you got. That man on TV had over a hundred, and I just bet you're gonna beat him."

"All of 'em, huh?" Donald smiled full.

Rose Marie smiled too, glad she had relented and taken the time to string the wire for his hats. She figured she could live with a hundred baseball caps or more hanging in her dining room and hall if it helped him. She could handle that.

"Rose Ma-r-e-e." Donald leaned his head back and crooned her name out. "Sweet Rose Ma-r-e-e. You gotta promise me somethin'." His look turned intense, his eyes piercing.

"Promise you nothing, Donald Calain, absolutely nothing. I heard you yelling 'rape, rape,' when the nurses tried to get you into a gown for the operating room."

"They loved it!" His eyes glinted with the humor of a tease.

"You want to think they loved it. I wanted to drop right through the floor with all your carrying on. Just drop right out of sight." She tugged at the bed sheet, smoothing it in her exasperation.

Donald's smile faded as he continued. "Promise me, please promise no matter how turned around I get, that you'll keep talkin' to me."

"You don't listen now when I talk to you."

"Promise me you'll keep talkin' to me no matter what. Remember a long time ago, when I took you to a football game down to Morgantown. All of a sudden you were scared, and you wouldn't come down outta' the grandstand after the game."

Stacks of blue and gold bleachers, seemingly stretching to the sky, filled her memory as she whispered, "Yes. I remember."

Then, as she gained control of her voice, struggling through the dark recall of the day, she spoke louder. "Oh, yes. Yes, I remember well."

"I talked to you so you wouldn't be scared. Told you how I loved you. A real Romeo."

"I don't know what came over me." Was it the memory of that fright or the sense of cold even here in the hospital that made her shiver?

"Talked you outta' your scariness. Remember how you could see the river through the goal posts from the old stadium? And I told you how I felt like I wanted to run right through those old goal posts and dive into that big old river. I said I would take you to a ridge way high up on Cheat Mountain where the water on one side runs into the Potomac and on the other it's the very beginning of that river down there."

She saw his eyes water slightly, fading into the past.

"That little old spring becomes the Tygart River, and it joins up with the West Fork to make the big old Monongahela. I told you about the Indian name for the Monongahela." Donald repeated the name, rolling out the word, emphasizing each of the five syllables, "Mo-non-ga-he-la. 'River with the banks fallin' in.' That's what it means in Indian talk. "

Rose Marie joined him in the past, recalling watching him from where they were high in the grandstand, rocking herself gently back and forth, seated on a bleacher, trapped by her sudden fear. She remembered Donald softly cradling her in his arms, his mouth close to her ear, and his warm breath as he began to whisper the names of the rivers of West Virginia. Even in the hospital room, she heard his voice slowly building into a sing-song chant and the comfort he brought to her.

"Ohio, Mononogahela, Cheat, Shavers Fork, Gandy, Laurel Fork, Black Fork, Tygart, Buckhannon, Galley, Big Kanawha, Little Kanawha, Potomac, Shenandoah, Stony, Greenbrier, Bluestone, Tug Fork, Elk." He had paused and then continued, "Singapore."

"Singapore!" Rose Marie had looked at him as though he had lost his senses. "Singapore isn't a river. It's a city."

Donald grinned. "Well, honey, I know that. I kinda run out of rivers and old Singapore popped outta' my mouth. No thought to it. Singapore had to be said, I reckon, so I said it."

"Oh, you clown. You silly, wonderful clown." Rose Marie laughed. And with her laughter all her fear suddenly vanished. What had kept her crouched high in the stands, unable to descend, was just as quickly gone.

She remembered how he gently helped her to stand and then, as they slowly climbed down the bleachers, he noted each row of the bleachers with the name of a river until he led her safely to the cinder track beside the football field.

As soon as they were down, Donald insisted they climb back up into the bleachers so she could prove to herself that she was no longer afraid. She agreed, feeling with Donald she could accomplish anything. When they stood there, high in the grandstand, he folded his arms about her, drawing her close and asked her to marry him.

With an unsuccessful marriage behind each of them, they stood there, two lonely, forty-year-olds holding each other in the stands at Mountaineer Field. They hugged each other tightly and laughed at the joy of being together. Then, carefully, his arm around her waist, guiding her step by step, Donald helped her climb down once again.

That was forty years ago, and she still didn't know what had frightened her so on that autumn afternoon. The years had gone by so quickly and now, here they were, in a second floor room in the Davis Memorial Hospital, in their mid-eighties, Donald stricken with dementia.

Back to the present, she saw him straining at the cloth ties, his body arching off the bed, stretching toward her. "Are you listenin' to me? I told you on top of those bleachers that I'd never ask you anything again if you'd just marry me. But, of course,

I've asked you lots of things over the years. And now I'm breakin' that promise again. You hear me?"

Rose Marie nodded, her thoughts still lingering on that October day so long ago.

"You gotta keep talkin' to me no matter what...even when..." he stopped, his lips moving but without any sound, and she knew he was lost again. Donald fell back onto the pillows. "Damn." His voice faded into a whisper as he pulled at his restraints. "Damn it all to hell and back."

"Donald," Rose Marie's rising inflection warning against his swearing.

"See, now I forgot again." He jerked his restrained fist and punched at the bed rails.

"You was telling me to keep talking to you."

"Talkin'? Talkin'?" Donald squinted, and then closed his eyes tightly.

Rose Marie could see from the way his veins stood out on his forehead and from over forty years of studying his face that he was struggling to pull his mind back to the conversation. She sat very straight, telling herself to breath deeply, slowly, to stay in control and not to give over to tears. She hated it when he became so lost.

"Oh, God, if I could just do or say something to help him," she whispered. "Help me, guide me to help him, to be able to keep him with me for a while longer."

And then, as though in answer to her prayer, Donald turned to face her, his smile embracing her in its joy as he remembered. "Yes, keep talkin' to me, even when I've checked out of this right-now time."

"Oh, honey, of course I'll talk to you. You know that." She spoke slowly, controlling the mounting fear, which seemed to drop on her like a shroud.

Donald continued to gaze intently at her, his eyes slightly shadowed by the Yankee cap still tilted on his head. "You know, maybe somethin' will seep through." Then he was like a little kid again, begging for a candy. "Promise?"

"Yes. I promise."

"Just tell me what its like back on Cheat with the rhododendron in bloom. You will, won't you, Rosie?"

Rose Marie nodded, her hands clenched into tight little fists as she fought to keep herself calm. "Sure, honey, I'll talk to you, no matter what."

She suddenly yearned to feel his big hands holding her. She looked toward the door, and then gingerly bent over his bed, untying the restraints. "Oh, I'll talk to you, you big old bear. And I will beat up on you if you give the nurses any more hard times."

He turned to gaze out the window, and she knew he had stopped listening. His memory was once again blown across an unmarked landscape, riding on the winter light.

As tears escaped from her eyes, she massaged his wrists where the cloth ties had made tiny wagon tracks. "You looked great that day. Way back at the game when West Virginia beat Pitt. A great fool, too, but you looked so good running down the field between the goal posts after the victory. And you got me calmed and down all them steps and you got me to marry you."

Donald turned his head slowly to face her. His look was full of joy, as though returning from a great distance, back in her world for the moment.

Then he laughed like the old Donald she knew best, his new Yankee cap slightly askew. "Yeah, you foxed me into hitchin' up with you." He pulled his hand from her grasp and reached up to rub his thumb down her cheek, stealing a tear. "Your eyes don't need no wash so you just cut that out."

She leaned onto the bed and into his arms as he embraced her, hugging her close.

Trailing Arbutus

His great granddaughter's school down in Charleston wanted to celebrate the approaching presidential election and West Virginia's 125th anniversary by recalling family history. Jacob had remembered the old letter and suggested it for her assignment. Trouble was, he couldn't recall where the letter might be, and Nancy wasn't here to ask. Jacob had argued with his daughters who were leaning in support of Dukakis. "No. We should stick with Bush. He's been a good vice president, and he'll do a fine job as president."

He tried to think of his great granddaughter's name, but he couldn't remember. Damn. Getting old was a pain in the ass in more ways than just his bum knee and forgetting things.

Now, he wouldn't be climbing these awful stairs but for the morning's long search trying to find the letter. He stopped on the fourth step, sat down, rubbed his hands over his knee, and took several deep breaths as he mumbled, "Why, oh why didn't I ever put a hand rail in this stupid staircase?" He hadn't been upstairs in the old house for years. In fact he couldn't remember the last time he climbed the steep, enclosed stairway to the two bedrooms on the second floor. The old farmhouse dated from about 1850, before the Civil War. Now the town was growing, and the farmhouse was just beyond the city limits.

They had stopped using the second floor ages ago when the kids got married and left home. Oh, the bedrooms got used when family came for over nights, but Nancy had taken care of making the beds and all that so he never had the need to ascend until now.

Rested after his brief sit, he pulled himself to his feet and stumbled to the top of the stairs. He paused in the doorway to the larger of the two rooms. That's where he remembered last seeing the old trunk. Nancy had made the determination of putting it at the foot of the iron bedstead they had inherited from Jacob's grandfather. "The old bed and the trunk go together," she said.

There were four brass knobs, one topping each of the iron posts of the head and foot supports. He touched the closest knob and rubbed his thumb over and around the sphere, feeling the unevenness of the old brass. How old was the bed now? He figured it dated from about 1880, maybe earlier. Granddad had been the last of the old family and, at 92 the year he died, he hadn't remembered when he had gotten it or from whom.

"Well, you're old, we sure know that," Jacob muttered to the bed as he moved to search the trunk.

Carefully, he lifted the curved lid, propped it against the foot of the bed and lowered himself to sit on the braid rug. He rested a moment and then rose to his knees, wincing as he settled his weight onto his heels. He removed a big comforter and placed it on the rug. There were quilts and sheets and pillow cases neatly folded and stacked inside the trunk. He pushed them aside, searching for the envelope and the letter.

Finally, he rolled off his knees and stretched his legs as he sighed. "No letter here. Why would I think it's in here anyway? But where else to look?"

Jacob had spent the morning searching the downstairs of the house. First, he had looked through the dresser drawers and chest in their bedroom. Certainly that was the logical place to put it. Nancy had always been so organized with a place for everything. Jacob smiled as he recalled the rest of the old quote: *and everything in its place.* Then he had checked every drawer and niche in the desk in the hallway where Nancy kept all her record books, taxes, receipts and such. All this looking had not led to success. So, here he was in the big old bedroom on the second floor, sprawled on the floor and still searching.

As he lifted the last of the linens from the trunk, the sleeve, as it was called, was uncovered in the corner of the trunk. "Ah ha, maybe success at last." Jacob slid the narrow wooden cover off the oblong box. He saw bundles of papers held together with rubber bands. Carefully, he lifted the items and stacked them on the floor beside him. Rummaging through his find, he fingered old deeds, folders of faded photographs, a recipe notebook, lots of old post cards, and then, finally, a yellowed envelope tied with a faded pink ribbon.

A smile spread across his face as he placed the envelope in his lap. Gently he pulled at the pink bow. Then, ever so slowly since he knew it would be fragile with age, he pulled a single piece of paper from the old envelope. It was ruled and looked to be torn from a notebook. If this was the letter his great granddaughter wanted she would have a marvelous contribution to her project. Damn, if he could just remember her name.

He sat up straight and unfolded the page. The script was written boldly in large letters with curly cues at the ends of the words. That much he could see. If this was the letter he was looking for, it had been written by his great aunt on the day of his mother's birth 106 years ago in 1882.

"I wish Nancy could see this," he said and then laughed, "because I can't. Why did I leave my glasses downstairs?"

This morning marked the end of the third week that he had been alone. Three very long weeks filled mostly with sports programs on the TV and nights sleeping on the couch. His daughters had stayed for the first week after the funeral to help him. Dorothy, his oldest girl, with her love of soap and neatness, had washed every piece of linen in the house. "Twice," Jacob had laughed when he spoke with Ellen, his best friend Bill's widow.

Jacob thought of Ellen now as he sat among all the quilts and sheets on the floor beside the trunk. It was a long time since Bill had been killed, and Ellen had handled her grief with amazing strength. That was what Nancy had said, over and over, as she included Ellen in so much of their life.

"That's what you do," Nancy would say. "You can't replace the love that's lost but you can try to fill the survivor's daily life. At least as best you can." Nancy had done just that. The result being that Ellen had spent a good deal of time with them in the years since Bill's death.

Now that his daughters had gone and he was alone, he thought of Ellen a lot. She was pretty, he would give her that. She was still thin, not skinny, with none of that obesity which so many older women seemed to spread into. His Nancy had been like that, too. Thin and very aware of how she looked. Jacob remembered he had heard Nancy and Ellen discussing various berry yogurts one day. Nancy had eaten yogurt for lunch every day for years.

Jacob leaned back against the bed. The loss of Bill was such a needless accident. The release pin on the loader stuck, and Bill had crawled under the pile of logs on the trailer to see what was blocking it. The men had told him not to do this, that they should try to trigger the pin with a pole or shake it loose. But Bill was the boss and, against all good advice, he slipped under the load, sliding on the low, wheeled wagon. And then the pin released without any tampering at all. Bill was so badly crushed the casket was closed at the viewing.

Jacob and Bill had grown up as best friends, graduated high school in the same class, and hunted together for years. Jacob missed him every day. "I guess I always will," he had confided to Nancy.

Ellen had called Jacob twice since Nancy's funeral, asking him to dinner. He had refused the first time because the girls were still helping him. The second time she had called he was watching the Baltimore Orioles, and they were losing to the New York Mets. He had been in no mood to chitchat. But now, maybe he would call her. He needed to talk to someone who understood about loss. He was tired of yelling at the umpires on the TV anyway.

Jacob folded the paper and tucked it back into the envelope. He pushed the faded pink ribbon in beside it and laid the envelope on the bed. After replacing all the linens and quilts, trying to stack them neatly back into the old trunk, he closed the lid. Holding the envelope carefully in his left hand, he slowly shuffled to the stairwell and began the steep descent of the stairway.

Sliding his right hand along the wall for support, he stopped on the third step from the bottom, his attention caught by the narrow shaft of sunlight streaming into the dim stairwell. He sat on the step, placed the envelope gently beside him, and looked at the button on the wall. The button, in carpentry terms, was a fairly large, thin, wooden disc which, when slid to one side, revealed a good-sized hole in the wall. Jacob smiled as he recalled the various explanations for the hole. His favorite was that the original hole was quite small and was drilled by a bullet. A bullet which probably came from a pistol. The story was that the shot had been fired at a Rebel Captain as he was fleeing the farmhouse after a rendezvous with one of the daughters of the household. That was back during the last year of the Civil War when both armies had lived off the families in the area. Even today some hard feelings remained over the harsh treatment of the locals back then by the Yankees. So much so, that most of the men folk of the community supported any baseball team other than the New York Yankees.

Over the years, the little bullet hole had been poked and prodded until now it was sizable. When he and Nancy bought the house years ago, Jacob had cut a new button to cover the opening. Now he leaned over to peek though the hole and was surprised to see his nephew pulling into the driveway.

"Oh, boy," Jacob muttered. He had forgotten that his nephew, Henry, was coming up to target shoot with his new .22 rifle. Jacob slipped the button closed, painfully got up from the stair, picked up the letter, and headed for the kitchen.

Jacob dropped the letter on the table in the breakfast room and stepped through the door into the yard. How had he not remembered that he was to help Henry with his new rifle? "Oh, boy" he grumbled as he rounded the house and saw Henry pulling the sheathed rifle from the back seat of his car.

Jacob paused a moment and then walked to greet Henry in the driveway. "Howdy. Where's your mother? I thought she was coming with you."

"Company. She's got the preacher and some lady from the church visiting. She said tell you that she would be making some cornbread and bring it out to you."

"Well, that's right good of her. She knows I miss Nancy's cornbread as much as anything." Jacob took a step towards Henry's car. "Now, you got to understand. I'm not mad at you or nothing, but I have to do this."

"What?"

"This." Jacob reached his hand to slap the hood of Henry's car and then kicked the front tire closest to him.

"What? Why you hitting my car? What's wrong?"

"Henry, you're old enough to remember Bataan and the Philippines. Doug Marsh's boy was killed on the Bataan Death March. And your new car? It's Jap make, isn't it?"

"Oh, Uncle Jacob, that was a long time ago. And of course I remember Johnny Marsh. We were in the Scouts, and I delivered their paper when I had my paper route."

"He was their only son."

"I know. After Johnny died, Mrs. Marsh wouldn't answer the door. She'd pay the paper bill by the month and slip the money under the door mat. I don't think I ever saw her after Johnny got killed."

"You remember yet you help the Japs by buying their car?"

"Uncle Jacob, the war's over for a long time. I hear the new surgeon at the hospital in town is Japanese."

"That's a whole different ball game. He's helping folks. I'm told he's real good."

Henry clenched the rifle between his hands. "Yeah, it's a Japanese made car, and it's a good one. I get great mileage, and it's real roomy. I guess it's pretty fair between Japan and us. We buy their stuff, and they buy ours. You know?"

"I reckon, but I still won't have a Jap car. Or nothing else made over there that I know of. No matter what."

"Okay. That's your choice."

"That's right. That's my choice." Jacob tried to think of something else to say to Henry, something positive, but nothing came to mind.

Henry broke the silence. "Are you okay with helping me?" He held up the rifle.

"Sure. But I don't forget Pearl Harbor. The *West Virginia* was one of the ships bad hit that day."

"I know that. The mainmast is mounted right in front of Oglebay Hall on the downtown campus at Morgantown."

"It is? I didn't know that." Jacob cleared his throat and gave a little cough. "Well, that's nice that it's there to remind folks." He eyed the rifle. "Okay, let's give a look-see at your gun." Jacob reached for the gun and began to slip it out of its cover. "Oh. Nice one. Marlin. Good gun."

"Wal-Mart, can you believe it?"

"They have some good things. You can't shoot this at your place up in New York?"

"Sure I can, and that's why I bought it. I thought I ought to have a gun because I'm a way out in the country, and then there's all the porcupines. Do you know they tried to eat the new steps to my deck?"

"It's the salt. They want that tiny bit of salt that's left from the carpenter's hands. It's in the wood and unless you paint to cover it, they'll eat the whole darn house."

"And oil or whatever. Porcupines ate the tubing and wiring and half the motor out of my neighbor's car one night."

"Not the oil. Its's the salt from the mechanic's hands."

"If you say so. I thought they had an acquired taste for oil and rubber." Henry laughed. "I had to drive my neighbors back to the city. You know, I haven't shot a gun for thirty years or more. Not since I was in the Army. I want to play safe when I break it in."

"Well, let's go. I got a target in the garage. We can set up on the hill back of the shed. That way, we don't shoot across the road." Jacob, carrying the rifle, led the way up from the driveway and into the garage where he grabbed the target. They walked out and across the lawn. "You got the shells?"

"Yessir." Henry laughed and snapped a smart salute as he answered.

"This target has a few holes shot in it. Don't know when that's from but it'll do for us to start anyway."

Jacob walked to the rise of a hill in the back and to the side of the house. He slipped the target behind a splinter on an old stump a few feet up the bank. "Yes, sir, this'll do just fine. You want to load it up?"

Henry reached for the rifle. "Well, I'll try. I read the instructions but it's been a long time. You know we were timed in basic training and had to learn to dismantle and reassemble an M-1 in a given number of minutes. I did fine then. But I was twenty years old." Henry laughed. "Now, I'm all thumbs."

"Take your time and be careful. This ain't the Army. You know I never had to go. My being with the weather bureau was called essential, and Nancy and me had the young girls. Just as well. I hate to be told what to do and when to do it."

"I'm glad I went. Wouldn't change the experience for anything but I sure don't want to do it again. Of course I was lucky when I was in Korea. Personnel found out I could type and they pulled me off the front line and made me a company clerk. I belong to a veterans group in New York, and I get nightmares from some of the stories the guys tell about Viet Nam."

"Yeah, that was a mess, for sure. And now the whole Arab thing. It never let's up, you know? Okay, let me try it out." Jacob took the loaded rifle from Henry, aimed carefully, and then let off a round. He leaned toward the target and squinted. "Well, it looks like I hit it. Let me see where before you take a shot." Jacob handed the rifle to Henry and walked to look at the target. "Low and to the right. I can do better than that." He walked back to Henry and motioned for him to shoot. "You know, Henry, squeeze the trigger, don't pull, and aim a bit high since you're shooting uphill."

Henry squeezed off a round. "Ow. This little number has a kick."

"You wanna try my 12 gauge? It's like getting kicked by a mule unless you learn to give a little and ride with the recoil." Jacob walked to the target. "Hey, look at that. You beat me. Doggone. You don't need no coaching. Try again."

Henry fired off several more rounds, the flutter of the target signaling that he had made the hit. He walked to look at his shots. "Hey, Uncle Jacob. I don't know why I thought I needed help. You know, I'm doing all right."

"You're right to be wary. Most folks don't think twice about how to handle a gun. Every year we get someone shot during deer season. They just don't take the time to make sure its a deer they're aiming for."

"But the orange vests must show up, don't they?"

"You'd think so but maybe a lot of folks are color blind, you know? Let me get a can from the barn. Take a couple more shots but we need a new target."

Walking toward the barn, Jacob heard Henry taking two more shots. He didn't need to search too long to find a can. He muttered as he came out of the barn, "A helluva lot easier than finding that letter." Tin can in hand, he signaled for Henry to hold up shooting as he took down the target and set the can on top of the stump.

"Let me have a try." He took the rifle from Henry, aimed and fired. The tin can flew into the air. "I gotta prove I can still hold my own here with Sergeant York," he laughed as he handed Henry the gun and moved to reset the tin can. "All right, your turn."

The can tumbled into the tall grass with Henry's shot, which had flipped the can a bit of a distance from the stump. They combed through the grass and weeds looking for it.

"Why look at this. Just look here." Jacob's call was one of surprised delight as he knelt in the grass. Slowly, he held up a single sprig of trailing arbutus, its little pink blossoms a tiny waterfall of color in his hand. He stood and stretched his hand to Henry. "Will you look at this? Trailing arbutus right here in the back yard and me and Nancy spent years every spring hunting all along the Cheat for it. I'll be damned."

"Aunt Nancy's favorite flower. I remember her on every picnic looking for it."

"Yes, Nancy and about half of West Virginia." Jacob laughed. "It's hard as hell to find. There are clubs all over built around this little bloom. It's precious as gold to folks who love it."

"We even looked for it when I was a Boy Scout. We'd take it home to our moms. Mother always made a big to-do of putting it in a little vase in the center of the table. It's supposed to bring good luck to anyone who finds it."

"All these years and here it is, right in our own back yard. I can't tell you how many times we went over to Cheat and spent afternoons looking for it. It likes to hide, to have cover. You never see it out in the open."

"Yeah. You got to search for it."

Remembering Nancy's searching for the flower over the years, Jacob felt his eyes begin to tear. He turned from Henry, so he wouldn't see.

"And you can't transplant it. I tried. Mother was determined to have it in her garden but no such luck. Now she settles for finding it once in a blue moon."

"Make sure you tell her about it's growing right here in my backyard. Well, not exactly the yard but up on the hill a ways."

"The soil must be right for it there," Henry said.

"I'm going to put this little lady in some water." Jacob wiped his eyes with the back of his hand and started toward the house. "You want to shoot your gun any more?" he called over his shoulder at the bottom of the hill.

"No, I think I'm okay with the rifle now. I just needed someone with me. A little reassurance was all."

Jacob turned to face him. "You want a cup of coffee? A Coke? Anything? I forget to be a good host just like I forget a lot of things."

"Thanks, Uncle Jacob. I got to get goin'. It's a short trip for me, and I promised to take Mother shopping."

"Be a good son and bring your mother out to see me before you go back to New York."

"I'll do that. We'll call you first. Thanks for your help with the rifle. Don't tell anyone I was such a baby about breaking it in."

"Nothing baby about being careful, and it was a pleasure." Jacob gave a hearty laugh. "And look what we discovered." He held up the flower. "You're still a good shot, and we found the trailing arbutus. Why, with seein' you and all it's been an awful good day."

Jacob watched Henry walk to his car, put the rifle in the trunk of his car, and climb into the driver's seat. He rolled down the window and waved as he slowly pulled out of the driveway.

"Take good care of that Jap car," Jacob called and waved goodbye.

Favoring his bum knee, Jacob crossed the yard to the house. He got a glass, filled it with water, and set the trailing arbutus on the table in the breakfast nook. Spying the envelope dropped there earlier, he pulled out a chair and eased into it, groaning at the effort. Slipping on his glasses, he squinted through them, and then took them off. He looked for something to wipe the lens. With a shrug, he tugged at his shirt and cleaned the glasses on his shirttail. Then, ever so carefully, he slipped the letter out of the envelope.

April 10, 1882

My Dear Addie,

It's Monday morning and I got a load of wash soaking, but I'll take a minute to write and send you my best wishes for an easy time. Hank's at work of course and the kids are in school except for the baby. He's still coughing some but I think the worst is over. Dr. Thompson got the fever down. He's so kind and wouldn't charge us for coming out here to the farm.

If I get this in the mail right now, in time for the noon train, you'll have it tomorrow which should be your big day. Of course, you may be having the new baby right now for all I know. I think it will be a boy because you're carrying low. But whether a boy or a girl, I've got two paper roses for you. A navy blue and a real pale pink. They're right nice from

Montgomery Ward. Hank got a little raise at the pail factory and he let me order some things. With both, you'll have the right color whether a boy or a girl. I got a purple lilac for my old straw hat and it'll look good as new with the flower.

Cousin Clara's oldest boy, Jeb, run off last week with two of his friends to join the Marines. Wilfred says he's never to set foot in the house again. I told Clara not to fret. When Jeb comes home on leave all decked out with ribbons on his chest, I bet you Wilfred will be the first one to say, "Look at my boy!" A uniform can make all the difference in the world.

I'm praying for you. I'll catch the late train tomorrow to come help you for a few days. The kids are old enough to keep house for Hank while I'm gone. Of course, I'll bring the baby. And I did like you asked. I made a list of all the family names. That is, as far back as I can remember and what I could find in the old Bible.

The Lord be with you.

Your loving sister,

Susan

Jacob read the letter again, sitting quietly, remembering his mother, his grandmother Addie and his Great Aunt Susan. With a soft smile curling his lips, he rasped, "You know I just bet Ellen would like to read this letter before I send it off to Charleston. And I know she'll want to hear about my finding the trailing arbutus. Yes sir, I know she would. I'll call her and ask her to dinner. The Old Inn is good, and I do like their steaks. Yes sir, I'll do just that. Oh, boy, here I go again, talking to myself," he laughed.

Jacob folded the letter carefully and returned it to the envelope, looping the pink ribbon about it. He leaned the letter against the glass holding the flower. Looking at the trailing arbutus, he hesitated a moment, then carefully lifted the sprig out of the glass. Carrying it into the bedroom, he gently placed it on Nancy's pillow.

Groaning a little, he sat on the bed and studied the flower. "Look at that. I never noticed before but the buds look like the little fists of a baby. All curled up tight. They're waitin' for just the right time, that secret signal to open to the world."

After a moment, he adjusted the trailing arbutus a bit, as though finding just the right place for it on Nancy's pillow.

"Oh, boy," he muttered as he got up slowly. Walking around the bed, Jacob turned down the cover on first Nancy's side, and then his. Slowly, sitting again, reaching to untie and then loosen his laces, he kicked off his boots. He stretched out on the bed, sighing as he sank into the softness of the comforter. Sleepily, he mused, "It's been a full day, a little shut eye before microwaving my supper won't hurt none. It's one of my favorites, Shrimp with Chinese vegetables."

He reached, blindly, for the sprig of trailing arbutus on Nancy's pillow. Retrieving it, gently cupping it in his hands, he yawned and stretched, making a nest on the thick quilt. Fighting to keep his eyes open, he pulled Nancy's pillow into his arms, careful not to crush the little flower. The pillow still smelled of her powder. He smiled as he recalled the name, *Evening In Paris*, the scent she had used for years.

"I found the trailing arbutus right in our back yard and brought a sprig in here for you. You know, Nancy, I've been sleeping on the couch in the living room since I lost you. Tonight, I think I'll sleep in here. Yeah. That's what I'll do." His words were slurred as he closed his eyes and drifted quickly into his before supper nap.

Maybe it was the warmth of Jacob's hand or perhaps it was just their time, for two of the little buds of the trailing arbutus opened in bloom.

Maple Marinade

Carl smiled as he opened the box of Christmas decorations and pulled out Olive's string of lights.

"Maple marinade," he whispered and laughed that he had actually uttered the words. Sorting out the various lights, he thought of that snowy drive two years ago. Try as he might to shut them out, memories seemed to come to him more readily as the time passed. He had learned to let them in, enjoy the memory, and not fight against them. Softly, he whispered again, "Maple marinade," as he began to tighten each light on the cord.

Stephen, his nephew, padded into the living room. "You say something?"

The question startled Carl. He had forgotten for the moment that Stephen was spending the holiday with him at his apartment in Florida. The visit was a present to Stephen for his coming college graduation and fulfilled the family's insistence that Carl not be alone for the holiday.

"No, I was just remembering. You can help me with the lights on the balcony later, okay?"

"Sure, call me. I'm going to work on my paper for a bit." With a wave of his hand, Stephen headed back to his room.

In silence, Carl continued to slowly tighten each bulb on Olive's string of lights as he recalled Christmas two years earlier.

It had been a bitterly cold winter and he and Olive had debated whether to brave the drive from Washington to spend Christmas at the cabin in West Virginia. The trip over the mountains in winter was a challenge and could be dangerous. It was the thought of the big fireplace and a roaring fire that had helped them make the final decision.

Safely at the cabin, Carl unloaded the last bit of firewood into the covered bin on the porch. He stomped his boots to shake off the icy snow and then scraped the soles on the edge of the porch. The snow was now over a foot deep and, according to the weather report, there was more to come.

"It's certainly gonna be a white Christmas," Carl said to Tygart, the old German Shepherd still following him wherever he went despite his advanced age and the arthritis that made his legs shake. Tygart whined and Carl helped him up the porch steps.

"Poor old fella," he gently scratched under his chin.

Tygart thanked him with a few licks.

In the hall, Carl wiped Tygart's feet with a towel. "There you go, old man. A night in front of the fire will make me and you feel just fine again."

Just then Olive called from the kitchen, "Hold it, Carl. I need you to go to the store for me."

Carl wiped his feet on the rug and walked down the short hallway to the kitchen. He felt the welcome warmth of the big room, glad to be home and out of the cold. "What? You want me to drive all the way back into town in this weather?"

Carl headed for the fireplace where Olive had a bright blaze going. He had designed the big room, which some folks now referred to as a Great Room. When Carl built it forty years earlier, he had simply wanted a room that enabled Olive to cook and still be a part of everything. It worked beautifully. A long counter separated the open kitchen from the dining area. The huge slate fireplace gave light and heat to both diners and folks watching the big TV screen at the far end of the room. As always, he cast an admiring glance at his design as he sat on the hearth.

"Maple marinade. I forgot to get it this morning."

"What the hell do we need maple marinade for?

"To soak your head." Olive's voice was tired, but her humor was not diminished. Then with just a bit of an edge, she added, "For your Christmas turkey tomorrow."

"Do we have to have it? Your turkey will be just fine without some fancy doings. It's going to be dark soon."

"I know. I would have asked you earlier, but you weren't home yet." Olive's tone grew softer. "I'm sorry to have to ask you. I know it's bad out there."

"It's snowing like crazy. The road was plowed, but it'll need it again right soon if this keeps up."

"Take Tygart. That way in case you slide off the road you'll have company to talk to." She laughed that soft, forgiving, beautiful sound that began with a low chuckle and grew into a lilting laugh that turned Carl to mush every time, even after all these years.

Carl sighed. "Come on, fella. The old girl wants some maple marinade, which I have never heard of. We may wreck the car, but the turkey will be cooked the way she wants. Come on."

"Thanks, sweetheart," Olive called.

Carl watched as Tygart struggled to his feet and stumbled toward him, his tail wagging in a low sweep. He knew that many German Shepherds had back leg problems as they aged and had hoped Tygart would be spared. Tygart had been a gangling puppy at the pound when they discovered him almost fifteen years ago, and he had proved irresistible. They never regretted their decision to give him a home.

Carl often thought of the troubles Olive and Tygart were facing in their old ages. Olive was fighting a long battle with cancer. Two surgeries had sapped her energy but had not dampened her spirit. She refused to limit her activities as the doctor ordered and Carl, trying not to call attention to the fact, did all he could to make things easier for her. He helped in every way possible until she sometimes scolded him by declaring, "I can do it. Let me alone. I'm not helpless." When she did ask him to do something, he made sure to protest some—just a little so she would not suspect that he was coddling her.

And now, of course he would drive through the snow on the icy roads to fetch her maple marinade, whatever the hell that was. Fifty years together and this was the first he'd heard of maple marinade. The people at the store would know what it was anyway. He didn't want to ask Olive in case she'd be upset with him for not listening to her some other time when she had talked of it. With a pretend grumble, and Tygart padding quietly after him, he walked to the hall where he had hung his heavy jacket and cap.

Olive came up behind them, holding a bandana. "Be careful. The roads will be slippery. I'm glad we had George plow. I hope some of the ashes will be a help on the driveway." She stooped to tie a bright, red handkerchief around Tygart's neck and then reached to give Carl a quick kiss on the cheek. "I love you. Drive slow. Don't rush. I'll have some of the venison soup ready when you get back."

"Love you, too. Where's the marinade at the store?"

"Along the wall with all the other spices, olive oils, and dressings. You'll see. It will have a dark green label." Olive switched on the porch and driveway lights.

Carl led Tygart carefully toward the car through the snow, smiling that he was able to help his Olive.

The first mile of the nine was a dirt road and their neighbor, George, had plowed it.

"Good man," Carl whispered and flashed his lights as he passed George on his plow where he was turning at the junction with the highway. The highway's four lanes had been plowed as well, but the lanes nearer the center were piling up again as drivers stuck close to the side. Carl drove slowly, keeping a good distance behind the taillights in front of him.

He scratchd Tygard on his head, "Gonna be a slow ride, my friend."

Tygart wagged his tail in response.

At the Kroger checkout, Carl said, "You guys staying open in all this?"

Sarah, who Carl called the old clerk, nodded. "We're closing a bit early. It's Christmas Eve, but we've all got to get home, too. Course, we want to be here for folks that needs last minute things. Like you." Sarah laughed. "We got to beat Santa, and he may be early what with all this weather."

Carl smiled his thanks, murmured, "Merry Christmas," and pushed through the door and out into the blowing snow.

In the car he placed the little bag with the marinade on the seat beside Tygart. "I thought it was gonna be hard to find, but it was right where Olive said with the dark green label. Watch that for me, okay? Don't want it to break 'cause we ain't going back for another."

Tygart thumped his tail and struggled to look out the window as Carl pulled out of the parking lot into the deserted street. The few Christmas lights on the lamp posts were swinging wildly in the wind and snow. Carl eased onto the highway for the trip back to the cabin.

It would be a slow and slippery drive, and he bit his lip to stop a curse at all marinades. Carl thought of Olive and that eased his anger at the storm. She was all he had. Well, except for Tygart. They had not been blessed with children, and now Carl was talking of giving up the cabin to his younger brother, his only close relative. He was in favor of a move to Florida but every time he mentioned it, Olive protested. So, here he was with Tygart and bottle of marinade and a very slow, difficult drive home.

Carl reached to rub Tygart's ears, a reassurance that he was not alone. Being a retired history teacher, Carl had named the dog after the river which in turn had been named after the first settler west of the Alleghenies. The arrival of the Tygart and Files' families was not welcomed in the valley that was a choice hunting ground for the Indians. In the late fall of 1753, they attacked the Files' cabin and murdered seven of the family. One boy had been across the creek and knowing he could not possibly save his family, ran to warn the Tygarts two miles up river. They escaped over an Indian trail by way of Fishing Hawk to the South Branch which was more settled and had several forts.

Carl loved telling the story of the Tygarts and the Files, and Olive good-naturedly warned all visitors to their cabin on Files Creek, "Don't get him started. We'll be here all night and still fighting the French and Indian War at breakfast."

Carl had been one of the first to buy land and build a cabin on Files Creek right after he was discharged from the Army in 1945. He had grown up and gone to school in the valley. His family was one of the so called old families who had settled along the Tygart River before the Revolution.

In 1945, there was only a dirt road along the creek and over the mountain. Now, all the possible building sites had been sold and Carl was grateful for his few acres which still gave him a sense of being *in the woods.*

Without taking his eyes off the road, Carl reached his right hand to scratch Tygart's head. "We've come a long way since 1753, fella. A long, long way. And no Indians, just a helluva lot of snow. You would have warned us of the Indians, I sure know that." He laughed as Tygart barked, then reached to lick his hand.

Carl did better than he had possibly imagined. The drive was tedious but not as slippery, it seemed, as the trip into the village had been. George had done a good job plowing the dirt road, and Carl slowed to a crawl as he neared his driveway. It was a right turn and too sharp for safety in this weather, so Carl drove a few feet ahead to his neighbor's driveway. There he turned around and headed back for the steep descent to the cabin. Olive's wish held for Carl could still see some of the ashes he had scattered earlier in the day in his now bright lights. He shifted into low gear for the steep incline and as he did, Tygart whined and sat up beside him.

Carl laughed. "How do you know we're here, boy? Even in the dark?"

Once down the incline, the driveway followed an old logging road about two hundred feet due south until it made a sharp left turn. Then it traveled along the fence line on down to the cabin by the creek.

As soon as Carl turned the corner he saw the lights. He braked and stared at the Christmas lights that decorated the front porch. "How in hell did she do that in this weather and weak as she's getting to be?"

Of course, he realized, that was her reason for his trip into the village for the maple marinade. The excuse to get him out of the house because she had not gotten the lights up before his late afternoon return. Carl reasoned, murmuring to Tygart, "The old girl's clever plot worked for she has completely surprised me with the Christmas lights. Surprised you, too, I suspect."

He drove slowly down the lane, thinking of the effort Olive must have made. She would have had to haul out the stepladder from the hall closet and maneuver it through the front door onto the porch. She was forbidden to climb even to the first rung. But she must have managed for the lights were strung all the away around the front door and the porch window.

He pulled under the carport and turned off the motor. "My, God. She did that for me." He blinked away tears and reached to pat Tygart who waited to be helped out of the car.

"It's seventy degrees and no snow down here but it's still Christmas Eve." Carl chuckled as he straightened Olive's string of lights and then looped them over his shoulder. They were so long some of them trailed behind him as he started toward the front door.

Stephen came out of his room. "You ready for some help?"

"Grab that tail end there, would you"" Carl gestured.

Stephen picked up the lights, following Carl to the front door. "How old was Tygart anyway?"

"Sixteen or so. We were never exactly sure since he was a stray, and we got him at the shelter. But he was getting up there. German Shepherds don't normally live that long, but I think old Tygart didn't want to leave me."

"Dad showed me where you buried him at the cabin and the little grave marker with his name. That's nice. You didn't want another dog?"

"Can't have a dog here in this condo. A cat or a bird, but who wants one of them? Not me. No, Tygart was special. Very special. So I don't want another pet. Besides, I got enough to do taking care of myself."

"I didn't know that about no dogs here. I saw a woman with a dog this afternoon. Maybe it's one of those service dogs."

"That's Wanda and her seeing eye dog. He's allowed. He never barks anyway."

They opened the front door and stepped into the hallway.

"Aunt Olive always decorated so much for Christmas. I remember her putting red bows everywhere from when I was little."

"Yeah. You know, down here in Florida it's all palm trees and poinsettias. No snow. Pretty, but I still miss the cabin—some. Of course Olive never got to see them—the palms and all. Tygart neither. But I know Olive would have loved the warm weather and the pool and the bougainvillea. The bright red ones especially."

"You're right about that, and maybe the warm weather might have made her more comfortable. You know, Dad and Mom talk about her a lot. You, too."

"Yeah, well. Things happen. Olive always had the lights around every front door we ever had. That is, wherever we were at Christmas. But you know," he shook the memory away, "it's Christmas Eve, and I have her string of lights." With Stephen's help, Carl looped the lights to frame the doorway.

"Okay, let's do the terrace. We'll fasten the reds along the top railing. Olive said Christmas wouldn't be Christmas without the color red. Santa's suit, poinsettias, and her red candles and bows all through the cabin. Folks driving across the 6th Avenue Bridge will enjoy the red lights here on the terrace. I'll turn them on when we go to the sports bar. Then you'll see how they look when we come home after the game."

Carl pulled a chair to the terrace railing and sat, motioning for Stephen to join him. As he talked, Carl looped the string of lights along the railing top. "Let me tell you about maple marinade and why I use it to cook with so often. We'll have it on the chicken tomorrow for Christmas dinner. I think you'll enjoy the flavor." With a gentle laugh, he continued. "There's a little story about all the Christmas lights and why they mean so much to me. You see, maple marinade was a favorite of Olive's. She used it to trick me once. Fooled me and Tygart good. I didn't much care for it at first, but it kinda grows on you."

Bringing Home the Colors

Icy paused at the doorway to the living room and pressed her clenched fist tight against her forehead. In her left hand she carried Robbie's French Horn.

"Icy?" Darrell was settled deep into his lounge chair when he looked up and saw her. "You all right?" He was running for the West Virginia state legislature and had been going over his speech to be delivered the next day at the Legion Hall.

"It's about Robbie's ashes." Robbie, their son, had been lost to AIDS early that spring of 1988. "I've gotten so used to them being here. With us. And now they'll be in the river."

"That's what he wanted." Darrell sat up.

"I know that. But just having them here. In the house. Well, I'll miss them."

"He loved Cheat River. I taught him to swim at Stuart's Park. Like my daddy taught me."

Darrell thought of the many Boy Scout hikes and all the camping he had done growing up during the Depression and World War II. There was a short cut to Cheat River and Stuart Park but a scary one. The railroad tunnel through Kelly Mountain was an early test for any boy in the area. It made the five mile hike a good mile and a half shorter. Darrell had conquered his fear and huddled into a shallow wall niche as the train roared by him when he was a Cub Scout.

He kept his adventure a secret from his parents, but friends spoke of his daring to their folks and word got back. Questioned by his dad as to the truth of the rumor, Darrell confessed. He had his butt booted good for being so foolhardy. Now, he smiled at the memory.

Darrell found out it was Bunny Atkinson who had tattled, and he challenged him to a fist fight. They each had a bloody nose by the time Mr. Holloway, the science teacher, discovered the fight back of the junior high school and separated them. Chores were assigned to each by the principal, and Darrell got his butt kicked again. Bunny and Darrell had become good friends and now, grown up and parents themselves, they golfed together.

"It's so pretty there." Icy spoke softly as she sat on the sofa, the horn beside her.

Darrell was taken out of his reverie by Icy's simple statement breaking into his thoughts. "Where are you going with his horn?" The cool, gleaming metal reminded him so much of Robbie. In his last two years of high school Robbie had been first chair.

"I thought I'd polish it."

"Today? We've got a lot going on." Darrell gestured to the notes spread across his lap. He tried to block the thought of whether Robbie had disobeyed and braved the tunnel as he had done. If he did, Darrell hadn't heard, and now he would never know.

Darrell wondered again, for maybe the umpteenth time, when did Robbie start thinking that he was attracted to other boys? Had Robbie experimented with his Boy Scout buddies? Darrell had never even dared the "You show me yours and I'll show you mine," when the other boys displayed themselves. The thoughts of his boyhood bothered him now as they hadn't before Robbie died. And, too, for the first time in years, he had dreamed of the Sergeant's drunken advances in Korea. The shocking, brutal attempt to seduce him had left a far deeper mark than he ever acknowledged. But Robbie's death had roused that long buried, sleeping nightmare.

Icy's voice rattled on. "It's something of Robbie's to be here with us after we scatter his ashes."

"What?" His reverie had blocked whatever Icy said. Taking a deep breath he made a stab at the lost conversation. "You know, I'll always think it was that Tom who got Robbie sick."

"Darrell, it doesn't matter. They're both gone now."

"Yeah." Darrell felt it best to end this turn of the conversation. "Time to finish up my speech. Hank and Judy and the kids will be coming over, and I've got to get this ready. You know Bush will be riding Reagan's coattails this fall." Darrell shook his head in disbelief. "I have a tough fight on my hands."

Icy continued her defense of Tom. "He was a nice boy. Good family and all."

Resigned, Darrell finally addressed his true feelings. "I didn't much care for him. I had to grit my teeth when he was here. He was just too, well, too, you know."

"No, I don't know. I liked him." Icy stopped as she tried to shush the persistent conversations playing over and over in her mind. They had begun the day after Robbie's death. Today, it was the voice of Tom's mother, inviting Darrell and her to Oregon. "If you come west, you must stay with us. Robbie was such a gracious host when we visited in New York City last spring." Icy pushed her fingers, hard, against her temples and murmured, "Oh, my."

"Are you okay?" Darrell's question revealed his concern.

Using her index finger Icy traced the big bell of the French Horn nestled in her arms. "I'm fine. Tom's parents are both teachers. Like you. Out in Portland."

"I know that. But why did Robbie have to bring him here?"

"They were together."

"I could never figure out how that boy got through service."

"Like all the other boys got through it. He was a soldier." There was starch in her reply. After all, Icy had been defending Robbie to his dad as long as she could remember.

Darrell had used the word "neat" to describe Tom in a conversation with Robbie. "He's a little too neat, don't you think?"

"If you mean precise, yes, I guess he is. He's a painter," and Robbie had walked away before Darrell could comment further.

Darrell felt like he was walking on eggs the entire time the two of them were visiting. How could this happen to his only son. Queer? Darrell hated that word, but he also hated to even think the term homosexual. And when Robbie confided to him that he was gay, that word, too, became difficult.

"Daddy, it's the way he was born. He's still the same son, the little brother I'm so proud of." Judy, backed up by Hank, tried to soften the obvious shock it had been to Darrell.

Again, Darrell's train of thought was punctured by Icy as she rattled on. "Robbie never talked much about Vietnam. They both survived that awful mess and still died so young. Oh, Darrell." Icy started to cry.

Darrell knew this would happen. Too often he had witnessed Icy's habit of worrying a subject, shaking it like a dog would shake a stick. Pushing at the concern, picking at it until the only relief was in tears. It was not unexpected, and he was prepared. A bit anyway. "Hey, get over here. Come to Papa." Darrell opened his arms to embrace Icy.

Icy carefully laid the horn on the sofa cushion. She crossed the room and snuggled into Darrell's embrace. His touch always quieted her, even after all these years. "Oh, Darrell, why did it have to be him?"

"God's will, honey." It was a pat answer, and Darrell hated to use it. But what could he say? Cautiously, softly, he continued, "It's over, Icy, done with. Okay?"

"Sometimes I think I hear him call out to me. 'Mama, Mama,' like when he was little."

Icy dried her eyes and stopped crying. She hadn't told Darrell about the voices or the ghostly figures that appeared now and again to her. Last week when she stepped into his old room, bright with the afternoon sun, Robbie was sitting on the bed, a book spread across his lap. He had smiled at her, that broad, beaming smile that had been such a part of him and then, before she could say his name, he was gone. The quick vision had taken her breath away and she gasped, leaning against the door jamb for support. A book was open on the floor beside his bed and the counterpane rumpled as though someone had sat there. She remembered the sun, warm across her shoulders, as she stretched out her hand to call Robbie back into the room. Icy hadn't told Darrell about that either.

"You got to stop thinking about what was. Life goes on, Icy."

"Doctor Harrison said 'Time heals everything,' he reminded me of that. He's such a caring man."

"Are you gonna help me with my speech?"

"Of course. Let me hear what you've written. Now, imagine you're the president delivering the State of the Union speech."

Darrell laughed, "Icy, I'm running for State Legislature."

"So? It's still important. And don't rush."

"You gonna listen or preach?"

"Of course I'll listen. But stand up. That gives you more energy and presence."

"All right, all right." Darrell stood and dropped his notebook onto the chair. "Okay, now, here goes. There were two thousand of us guys saluting that grand old lady as we sailed into New York harbor. The first division to come home from Korea, to bring back the flag, stack arms, and fold the colors until the next time. Bringing Home The Colors, that's what's its called." Darrell paused, proud that he had gotten through the beginning of his speech. "So?"

"Well, Mr. Darrell Benson, I think I'm going to vote for you. That's a lovely start, and you do it good."

"That's to remind folks that I'm a veteran."

"You didn't tell them that *Life* magazine put it on their cover. I pasted it in my scrapbook. I was so proud of you. We all were. The Army was trying to get all you returning soldiers home by Easter, and everyone in the country had their fingers crossed."

"No time for all of that."

"You flew in that Sunday morning from Washington and when you stepped off the plane I handed you Judy. She was only six weeks old." Icy laughed. "You were so afraid you would drop her. Oh, such memories." Icy stopped, gave a little laugh again, and leaned to kiss Darrell on the cheek. "I do go on, don't I? I have a feeling you're going to win. I just know it."

"Anyway, then I have to get into the issues. The landfill and the new water plant and about the schools. A whole bunch of stuff I have on note cards. And about my volunteering instead of waiting to be drafted. Just like I'm stepping up now to represent folks in Charleston."

Icy laid out the cards on a small table in front of Darrell. They studied them, briefly, and Icy switched two of them. "I think talking about your years as a teacher works better at the closing. Don't you?"

"Maybe, let me see." Darrell perused the cards, touching them one at a time as he silently pondered her suggestion. Then, remembering, he blurted, "Oh, did I tell you they've gotten three Veterans to be on the stand with me? One each from the Army, Navy and Marines. How about that?"

"You should get all the veterans' votes."

"I'll wear my Army cap, but they'll be in full dress uniform."

"I don't think your friend, your opponent, Mr. Miles Callison, served, did he?" Icy had emphasized "opponent."

"He had a medical exemption. But Miles has the money and the coal interest on his side."

"You got lots of teachers. And veterans. They all know you from the Legion Hall."

Darrell pictured the Legion Hall and thought of the many meetings and social gatherings over the years. In some ways, the Legion Hall was the center of life for the town, certainly for the men and women who were veterans. When he joined after his discharge in 1954, the oldest members had served in World War I.

One of them, John Barton, an older friend of his father, had been an early hero to him when he was growing up. John was an old man when Darrell was a boy, and many times he had listened to the stories of the trench warfare of World War I. John was a teller at the bank and vacationed every year with Mason Whitehead, the county clerk. John lived down the road and Darrell would see him limp off to the liquor store every Friday afternoon after the bank closed. With his little wicker basket hanging from his arm, he would pick up two bottles of wine. Always two, never more. Once, Darrell heard his dad remark to his mother, "That's the joy kick for his weekend." When Darrell had asked what that meant, he was scolded by his father who said, "His wine and who he shares it with is his business. You pay him respect. He was wounded in France." Of course, Darrell had heard the whispers about the two old bachelors and their vacation together every summer at Ocean City, Maryland. John lived with his mother until she passed on and Mason lived in the old family farmhouse at the edge of town. But it was an open secret that John was often seen early mornings making his way from Mason's house into the bank for the day's work.

In response to neighbors questioning his early morning walk into town, John would say "We gardened late last night so I stayed over." A simple, direct statement which never changed over the years.

Now, Darrell realized that their relationship probably had been just what folks speculated. Yet no one bothered them, and they were both deacons in the Presbyterian Church.

Darrell wondered if Robbie and Tom would have been like the two old bachelors if they had lived? He was jolted back to the present by the sudden appearance of their daughter, Judy.

Judy burst into the house, shouting, her voice shrill, "Daddy, Daddy, someone painted the garage. Red paint all over the side."

"What are you talking about?"

"Paint, Daddy. Big letters in red on the garage."

Hank, Judy's husband, angrily stepped into the living room. "I guess you haven't been outside this morning. It must have been done last night."

"Paint? On the garage?" Darrell dropped his notes and hurried out the door with Hank close behind.

Icy, confused, asked, "What? Someone painted our garage?"

"No, Mama. Just big letters on the side facing the road."

"Let me see." Icy pushed past Judy and followed the men out of the house.

Icy, supported by Judy, came back into the house first. They were soon followed by Darrell and Hank.

Quietly, Icy asked, "Why would someone do that? Those big letters smeared all over the side of our garage."

Darrell cursed, "Damn, damn damn. You can see where they got out of the car 'cause there's paint dribbled all across the grass."

Hank's anger matched Darrell's as he blurted, "It's the damn Republicans. Miles Callison's men. A sneaky, cheap trick! I've never seen anything like this before. Ever!"

"Why AIDS do you think?" Darrell looked around helplessly, truly baffled.

"Oh, Daddy. It's about Robbie."

"We said pneumonia in the newspaper. That's what took him. The doctor even wrote that on the death certificate."

"Yes, Daddy," Judy explained. "Pneumonia brought about by AIDS."

"People know about Robbie? I mean, no one's said anything like that to me."

"Oh, Daddy, of course they haven't. And no one would. But everyone knew about Robbie. Have known for years."

Carefully, Hank said, "I guess everyone knew Robbie was gay and that he died far too young. And, Darrell, you're running for State Legislature. Dirty tricks are dirty tricks. As they say, 'all's fair in love and war and politics'."

The words "love and war" hit Darrell like he'd been punched in the stomach. He got a little sick every time he remembered his one sexual encounter with a man. It was his first week on the front line in Korea, and he had been standing guard duty when the First Sergeant of the company suddenly appeared out of the darkness. Darrell was totally unprepared when the sergeant slammed him against the sandbagged bunker with such force Darrell's helmet fell off. The sergeant had slapped him across the face, grabbed his throat with both hands and hissed, "One word and you're court-martialed. My word against yours." The sergeant whispered, his whiskey breath overpowering as his mouth pressed close to Darrell's ear, "Say one word and you better head for North Korea 'cause I'll testify you're a fag." Darrell felt his fly roughly pulled open and the hot mouth of the sergeant quickly slobbering over him. He had been so surprised, so frightened at the sergeant's assault, that sex was beyond him.

The sergeant had avoided Darrell after that night and rotated back to the states the week after the war ended in July. Troops in the Company compared notes and found that several of them had been raped by the sergeant. Not one of the young men reported their encounter to the company commander, and it was known that some had welcomed the sexual release the sergeant offered. He remembered guys talking of several regulars from the motor pool. This had been a shocking revelation to Darrell, and he never spoke of it other than to buddies in his company. Once he found out about Robbie's sexuality, the sergeant had twice appeared in Darrell's dreams. What haunted him was the mental picture now and again of Robbie with some young man. Finally, Darrell had talked with Doctor Harrison who had suggested therapy. That helped but

Darrell never told Icy. Since Robbie's death, the dream had happened once again. He had awakened, sweaty and aroused, and the arousal was even more alarming now for in his dream the sergeant looked like Robbie's friend, Tom.

"Folks burned those little boys' house down in Florida." Hank's voice broke Darrell's reverie.

"What?" Darrell brushed his hand across his brow, in an effort to erase the Sergeant's image.

Hank, always patient, explained. "Darrell, down in Florida, neighbors burned the house of those three brothers who have AIDS. The little boys got it through transfusions."

"How do you know that?" Darrell's words tumbled out as he tried to blank the sergeant from his thoughts.

"Susan, my cousin, lives in Sarasota about forty miles away. The brothers are hemophiliacs. The school board said they could attend school and folks burned the house. It's been in the news."

"Miles Callison wouldn't sign off on something like this. He's a politician but he's a good man. Of course, there are folks with vested interests, and their money is riding with whoever wins. But burn a house, that wouldn't happen here."

"Daddy, Annie came home from a sleepover last week crying about AIDS. She said the girls asked her if she had it because of her Uncle Robbie. I tired to reassure her and explained that the illness wasn't passed by touching or drinking after someone."

"When I came home that evening, I told her the same thing. Obviously, folks are talking. Even little kids like Annie."

Darrell looked at Icy and Judy and finally back at Hank. "Annie's only a little girl. She shouldn't have to think about things like AIDS."

"Amen to that." Hank quickly added, "Dealing with her Uncle Robbie's death is more than enough for a ten year old."

"You know, Hank, I tried to persuade Robbie to wait and go to Morgantown, but he enlisted right after graduating high school. He said, 'No, Dad. I want to help. You volunteered against your dad's wishes.' Robbie had laughed. 'Why don't we make volunteering a family tradition?'"

"I didn't know that, Darrell. I do know I'm damn proud of my brother-in-law. Here he was, sick as all hell, but still helping others and still protesting."

Icy took Judy's hand. "We taught him and Judy to help others when they could."

Judy turned to Hank, "Are you going to tell them or shall I?"

"Go ahead. You tell them. He gave them to you."

"Tell us what?" Darrell, still lost in the unwelcome recall of the incident in Korea, heard Judy's voice as though coming from far away.

"Hank, make sure I get it right. Mom, Daddy, you know we were in New York for Hank's business meeting this past February. We didn't realize how sick Robbie was until we saw him in the hospital." Judy hesitated, then, softly, she went on. "He reached under his pillow and pulled out a small linen bag. He asked me to open it. There was a picture of Tom and him at a campfire. And there were his dog tags, two sets. He asked me to give them to you."

Hank interrupted, "You forgot to tell them Tom died Christmas Eve. Tom's parents had flown in to take both Tom and Robbie back to Oregon to recover. But, it wasn't meant to be."

Judy opened her purse and pulled out the dog tags. "Someday, not now, but someday, Daddy, I hope you'll give these to Annie and Peter. They adored their Uncle Robbie."

"Oh, my. Darrell, let me see." Icy took a chain of the tags and carefully slipped it over her head. "I'll wear these this afternoon. For his memorial."

Judy started to cry, unable to continue.

Hank picked up the story. "He told us The Gay Veterans Group in New York City had been granted permission to place a wreath at the Tomb of the Unknown Soldier. Robbie said when folks saw the gay banner, some of them turned their backs. The group placed the wreath the morning of the Gay March on Washington last October. We caught a bit of it on TV watching it to see if we could spot Robbie."

"Folks turned their back on them?" Darrell stared at Hank in disbelief.

"What gets me is that every single one of those veterans had to lie about their sexuality in order to serve." Hank's voice was harsh as he continued. "It's a damn good thing I wasn't there."

"I don't know what to say. Thank you, certainly, for telling me." Darrell remembered the picture of Robbie and Tom. It had been taken on one of their hiking trips. The two of them, dressed for the woods, smiling at each other, their faces lit by a brightly burning camp fire. He had made Icy put it away, out of sight. Now, that picture flooded his vision.

"Daddy, Robbie held my hand, real tight, so tight it left a bruise." Judy stopped, took a deep breath, and continued. "Oh, Daddy, I am so proud of him. He was helping guys write their Wills from his hospital bed." She started to cry again.

"Shh, shh." Hank looked at Darrell and then Icy. "I want to paint over those letters before we go. There's paint and brushes in the garage, right?"

"Wait, Hank. Give me a minute or two." Darrell stood slowly, a pair of the dog tags dangling in his hand. "Excuse me, I'll be right back." He strode to the hallway and his heavy footsteps marked his ascent of the stairs.

"He's upset. I should go help him." Icy started to get up.

"No, Mama." Judy reached to stop her mother. "Give him a little time. I know this has hit him hard."

"But, Hank, what about the kids? I have our picnic lunch all ready."

"They're with my mom. We'll pick them up on the way."

"How is Ethel? What's her doctor say?" Icy asked.

"Her doctor told her to lay off the gin before noon, and she'd be fine."

"What?" Shocked, Icy continued. "Ethel's drinking with her medication? Why, she knows better than to do that."

"Hank. Stop that." Judy wiped her eyes with a handkerchief, pulled out a hand mirror, and began to touch up her makeup. "Mom, he's kidding. She's doing just fine." Judy turned to Hank and playfully punched his nose with her powder puff. "You know, Mom worships you and believes your word is gospel."

"Oh, Hank, you cutup. I'm happy Ethel isn't drinking. Well, sometimes we do have a glass of wine. You know, when we meet for our needlepoint." Icy laughed, the most relaxed she had been all morning.

Darrell slowly walked back into the living room. He wore his Army cap, the other set of Robbie's dog tags about his neck, and carried the picture of Robbie and Tom. "I knew right where this was. I made Icy put it away. But we should have it here, with us, in the living room. You know?" He paused and sat beside Icy on the sofa. He gestured to the French Horn. "Icy, we'll polish this up later."

"Oh, can we? Judy, you remember, Robbie played first chair down at Morgantown."

"I knew that, too." Hank, grousing, went on. "Too bad the football team doesn't play football the way that band plays music."

Icy carefully traced the big bell of the horn. "We'll show this to the kids this evening. Remind them about the band."

"Maybe we can change Annie's mind about wanting a set of drums," Hank laughed.

"Hank, Judy," Darrell raised his voice to gain their attention. "Thank you for giving us Robbie's dog tags. And thank you for telling us about Arlington. It wasn't right for folks to turn their backs. Veterans are veterans. You know, we have to explain to Annie so she's not afraid. So she knows that her Uncle Robbie helped others, that he was a hero. That she won't get sick."

"Oh, Daddy, I know this is a lot to hit you with all at once. And today, of all days, when we're going to scatter Robbie's ashes."

"No, it's fine. I'm proud of him." Darrell hesitated, then continued. "Proud of Tom, too. They both served and were honorably discharged. You know, I've been so worried about my speech tomorrow. But what you told me about the wreath and all, well now I know what I need to say. About all of us working together. We don't have time to quarrel among ourselves. I want to tell them about Robbie volunteering, too. He lost the battle against AIDS, but he was helping other folks right to the end." Darrell stopped, unable to go on.

Hank stood. "Before we leave, I've got to do something about that paint on the garage."

"Oh, dear, the paint. I forgot about that." Icy looked at Darrell for an answer.

"Wait. Wait a minute." Darrell paused for a moment. "I've been thinking, folks ought to see the paint. Maybe this senseless vandalism will help people to be more understanding. You know? So, if you all say okay, let's leave it."

"Leave it?" Icy looked at Darrell, then at Judy. "What do you think?"

Judy nodded to Darrell, "Yes, Daddy."

Hank knelt beside Judy and quietly whispered, "Yes. Fine with me, too."

Darrell coughed, cleared his throat and placed his hand over Icy's on the French Horn. After a moment, his voice firm, he said, "Then we'll just leave it."